A Book of Emblems

A Book of Emblems

by
Page Nelson

based on
Adrian van de Venne's
Illustrations for the *Emblemata of Zinne-werck*
by
Johannes de Brunes (1624)

Edited and with an Introduction
by
William Ruminant

Another Sparrow
Press
2014

Published by Another Sparrow Press, the publishing branch
for fine arts and the humanities
of Passerine Inc., a global multi-media entertainment provider

ISBN: 978-0692238981

Cataloging-at-Publication Data
Nelson, Page, 1952-
A Book of Emblems: based on Adrian van de Venne's Illustrations for the *Emblemata of Zinne-werck* by Johannes de Brunes (1624) / by Page Nelson, edited and with an introduction by William Ruminant.
 1. Man-woman relationships — Fiction. 2. Emblemata of Zinne-werck — Influence.
 I. Ruminant, William. II. Title.
PS3546.E478B66 2014   2014
RDA-NEG8   CAP/NOTCIP

Revised edition

Book design by Jo-Anne Rosen, Petaluma, California

Cover art: from Adrian van de Venne's title page, *Emblemata of Zinne-werck*

"To the animals of the forest who speak no evil."

— Gertrude Kolmar, *Der Engel im Walde*

"I always recall the first chapter of an advanced maths textbook; 'arrangements, permutations, combinations', that's it really."

— *Claude Simon, interview*

"The point of demonstration is not the creation of illusion but explanation of an occurrence."

— Nicholas Mosley, *Catastrophe Practice*

"All stories begin in the middle because it is impossible to think of a beginning of time. There's this guy, see and there's this dame, okay? From here, there are always two questions: what's going to happen to them and how did they get there? Even the opening verse of the Bible is a vertical slash down the temporal continuum."

— Northrop Frye, *Notebook 52*

A single violin properly tunes the orchestra, five pitching in sequence makes one suspect the score is defective or lacking, that one isn't an auditor at a concert but a participant in a happening.

— *A Book of Emblems*

Due to a manufacturing intervention, the Afterword precedes the Introduction in some copies. The publisher regrets any inconvenience.

Contents

Afterword by Guy Mantis

The general editor, Dr William Ruminant, directing the full resources of his Institute, operating at the highest levels of textual terrain, could care less for the plein air scenics of mere biography. Yet as it happened, the unusually intractable texture of Page Nelson's manuscript meant that if it were to be coherently presented, it required klieg light illumination from living biographers, the few that knew him.

In the beaten path of youthful friendship, I was the first to expose him to ascendant art and major music. He confided that he had grown up in circumscribed circumstances and indeed, every empty ledger of his mental treasury indicated it was so. Under generous tutelage, he improved. His corvid curiosity was quick to peck at this and that. How unfortunate that this anxious energy metastasized over decades, culminating in his recent breakdown. I might have anticipated, should have known on that first evening when I gently placed the sapphire stylus in the vinyl grove invoking from the depth of silence, womb of imagination, Schubert's Death and the Maiden Quartet, that the intoxicant of great art can induce a straining clarification too intense for unstable spectators to handle even if the crisis, always precipitous, may take decades to eventualise. We pray for his full and rapid recovery.

His friends are left with the hard task of this fractured text, his sole and problematic legacy in our custodial hands. Dr. Ruminant had many questions about Nelson's project as he courageously struggled to organize the almost impossibly variant textual branchings. What I could supply, soberly, modestly, dutifully, were straight facts of the life even at the discomforting cost of my care for my friend's reputation. We now know how false, fallacious even as fiction was his adulterated testimony.

As to his distorted presentation of my person, I could be pained did I not recognize the delusional mind from which it originates. He says I was ugly (and if it so, would it not be more ugly to say so) when, as he knows, some have found my mental and physical attributes congenial. He characterizes me as ungenerous when, in this instance, his accurate account demonstrates how no one exercised themselves more to transport him from the vacant ground of his cultural ignorance to the visionary heights of the Sublime. He cynically patronizes Ruminant who has done everything to assist him, even referring the manuscript against his astringent judgment of its suitability to the attention of that brave little press, Another Sparrow. It is all very sad.

But less sad, not only for the improved emergent text, bravely fledged by Sparrow, but for the coming together of old friends once again in a selfless and harmonious partnership.

I especially want to recognize the author's long-term and, may I add, long suffering companion, Janet Nielson who conveyed the record of our friendship to Ruminant, midwived our collaboration, magnificently and magnanimously overcoming discomfiture about her own depiction in his book, which if true, violates every connubial confidence and if not, and it is not, is slanderous, for truth is truth and slander merely mean. It was gratifying for us, again joining hands around the body of our troubled friend, to insulate him if only belatedly from his blundering imbalances. The reader who has extended his indulgence as far as this Afterword will best appreciate our careful conservation of this wobbly and wandering text.

There was one other product from the rescue. In a deep heave of intuition, as all true inspiration is, I was aware of another performative imperative. Only I could do it. To produce a portrait that — more than a fair likeness — rectified the inner man, joining all the facets of his shattered life into unified aesthetic entity that honored his person and redeemed his failed, fractious project. This was my minor if fated labor, finished in a mere month, an object that after several weeks display in Houston's Exxon Mobile Gallery was acquired by a mid-western connoisseur-critic, a man of taste who tastefully wishes to remain anonymous. I offered the proceeds first to Janet. She graciously refused them. Then to the William Ruminant Institute for Textual and Editorial Studies, a healing facility best equipped to deal with ailing manuscripts such as painfully confuted my tragically aspirant friend. Ars longa, vita brevis.

Frequently Asked Questions, or, A Guide to the Perplexed (Author's Prologue)

Last night, between the exquisite sex dreams, these an unanticipated and lurid radio-erotic decay feature of a shrinking brain — the best encounters of my life, the idea of my next book came to me, a life guide to the perplexed, beginning with a series of *Frequently Asked Questions* and helpful answers. While all elements will not be relevant to all persons, there is something here for everyone.

What is the greatest book?
Shakespeare's Works; second place, the Oxford English Dictionary.

What is the greatest piece of music?
Bach's Art of Fugue, which can not only be played via the standard scansion but in reverse; also sideways, a multi-dimensional musical encoding that gives satisfaction no matter which way it is deciphered.

What is the most beautiful place on the planet?
Despite our every effort to ruin it by a vast simultaneous violation of over exposure and neglect, Venice, because La Serenissima integrates into her beauty a glistening, intestinal ugliness.

What was the greatest personal weapon?
The Turkish compound bow, its quick, accurate at range shots surpassing the effect of any western weapon until the invention the Martini-Henry, a reliable, fast firing, easily mass-manufactured breechloader in the 1870s. This changed the battlefield equation since any seventeen year old could be trained a competent shot in a week while the bow took a decade to master. The firearm also had a future in further development, the already perfected bow, none.

Is there any good about unilateral deafness?
Yes, the turning of the dead ear to what's unpleasant (i.e., meeting jabber, loud "music", bores). The most euphoniously denominated tumor, the cerebral bellopontine.

What is the most important thing in life?
Being born.

What is a dog's breakfast?
I have no idea aside from the obvious; something a dog eats in the morning. Traditionally, what was left over from the human dinner the night before, bits of bone, scarps of grizzle, vegetable residues such as carrot tops, good for the night stalking gaze hounds, *if any*.

In literary terms, this text is a dog's breakfast, not that supper would be any better. Should you want traditional literature or even nontraditional, there's is no lack of it – a smorgasbord of surplus, laid out for your selection. Item (serving suggestions), the thirty-two novels of Parcel Post, *Whorl and Poltise* or anything by Tallstory, *Fall Pire* by Vlad Sirin, *Humboldt's Rift* (oceanic geology, slow paced, convincingly if glacially narrated), the *King of Spain's Bible,* * honest, there is no end to the stuff, over ten million titles of fiction in English alone. But there is one and only one (or at least not so very many) dogs' breakfasts, which would be its ideal title (nomen est cognomen) except the image of a slobbering, mouthing dog, the sounds, smells, the skin crawling click of claws, disgusts me. Not that I dislike dogs, (they mean well no harm in their flat skulled way) only that the mix of curs and culture ("curture") is a bad one. There is great horse art and significant bird, cattle and cat art. There is no instance of great dog art. Literary investigations of the dog however, such as Kafka's, are not to be discounted. Nor should we forget that Rilke, most cat-like of men, pined poetically for a pooch.

What is the point of this?
I want to have the final word on certain *personal* matters.

And do these matters matter?
Except to me, not at all.

---

* [Editor's note: Daup. "Is the King of Spain's bible
an author? Cler. "Yes, and Corpus." Daup. "Sure, Corpus
was a Dutchman." Jonson, *Epicene*, II, ii.]

Should the reader (always assume one bemused/confused reader) continue?

To answer seriously and fairly, yes and no. Many things do not matter, are pointless in the way entertainments are pointless — "Slackers beat Polecats 22-17 at Home in Overtime." Thousands go to galleries to view color reflective chemical smeared on canvas, photonic radiation taken in at the eyes, reversed by the gelatinous lenses, rectified by the optic nerve, transmitted to the cerebellum opitcus, images that don't compute and won't be recalled by the dog's breakfast.

See an old man with a grey beard and a funny hat (*Mawkish. Try again.*) Observe an old man in a funny beard and a grey hat, an eldster who has lived and loved, known grief and grace, staggering with the burden of a last word, his dying declaration, a final judgment, bequeathing this promontory, this vista and vast surveying propinquity, music at the close. You will the possessor of the superior position. It is good to be on top. Only beware, he will conjure you. (Good prosperoic toast: "Conjure!" Superior to "Cheers.") Seriously, your choice, read or not.

Okay, let's put it this way, what else is this book attempting to achieve?

The avoidance of anesthetized tediousness, examples of which are the factualated fictions of almost any author you'd care to name, and the fictonalized facts of, say, James Slater's exquisitely composed memoirs. After reading a hundred pages of either, I weep with boredom. So beautiful! So boring! Heroically, I have resisted my own strong impulses to composed prose, I have tossed bits of narrative in like a (w)reckless salad maker. The result may be self-indulgent, incoherent, off-putting, but not, I pray, boring in the common gorgeous-gagging way; aesthetically tedious (oh, no-doubt!) *but ruefully, worn with a difference.*

What are we waiting for?
Death.

What is Death?

One is reminded of the analytic philosophical asshole (someone, btw, has just written "*A Taxonomy of Assholes*") who seriously remarked no one should fear death because no one ever actually experiences it. You're dead before you k(now) it! Who knew? Now death, the state of being dead, from the view point of consciousness is either a something or a nothing. Do you remember life before you were born? No, nothing. So you were dead before you were born. Q.E.D. Nothing to worry about.

Still there are the anomalous cases. Consider the investigations of Dr Ian Stevenson of the University of Virginia, conducted in India. A child is terrified of donkeys. She tells Stevenson that when she "was a child before" she was kicked by a donkey and died. She was living in a place called Gawan. Stevenson knows this is the native pronunciation of a place named Dawan, 400 miles away in Uttar Pradesh. He travels there, villagers still recall the case of the little girl killed by a donkey. Buddhists recall past lives all the time. Let's not make too much of it. Likely they are perceiving fragments of lives (the equivalent of a too receptive radio) and are sincere in the same way Christians testify to meeting the Virgin Mary in a cave. (Our Holy Mother discretely prefers caves to stadiums.) Best advice — as always, prepare for the worst, hope for the best. Some day we will know or not. The road back from Lourdes, strewn with crutches, sports not one artificial leg. Trust but verify. The fear of death at least keeps us busy. Yadda yadda.

Will you cut the comedy? Or at least cease the leaden persiflage?
Such facetiousness you say, never very funny to begin with, grows more than tiresome in extension. You would have me shed my baroque vestigiments, stand before you bare, the proverbial verbal forked radish; exposing cold scars and set dislocations, have me flail my skin to reveal a red heart turned pomegranate inside out so you can dissect my tragedies, triumphs and pluck out mine mystery.

What is the nature of reality?
Selected elements of Buddhism, Hegel, High Art and physics,

provide the best answer. For we have mined, travailed, found grains. Shifting and weighting them however involves a complex time consuming process with the only assurance a by no means certain result. We want an accessible and tractable answer to the problems of the material and spiritual, of mind and mind, our lives and deaths. And we want it now. While my belief is that after you die you are entirely non-existent, I am open to being pleasantly surprised in the matter. If it is the case that in this sliver of the electro-magnetic spectrum we are body-brain based physical creatures, it is by no means clear that "the physical" is reductively physical since our apprehension of matter and its functions, via matter, is part of what we are trying to define. (Never mind mathematics.) My sense is that "material" and "non material" are different ends of the same stick, that something we don't understand underlies our schema of dichotomies. Some would say this is beginning to sound like God. No, my intuition is inclined towards a supramundane substance, not a Supremo, a (meta) physics not a creed, with the really interesting situation being that in our highest exertions (experiments) of Love and Art we not only access this reality but as "artists" enhance it. My credo: (and we all believe something even if it is almost nothing – and most of us, too much of too little) let us live in a posture of openness to ourselves and others, extending a practical compassion extended to Nature as we occupy ourselves in the best work we are fitted to by our nobler natures and nurture. (This anticipates Frye who writes in his notebook "Art is not simply an identity of illusion and reality; its world is a material world, *an intelligible spiritual one.*")

Can farts put out fires?
Human flatulence is commonly composed of 30% carbon dioxide, 30% oxygen, 10% trace gases and, last considered, 30% nitrogen as chief suffocate; a higher proportion than in the atmosphere since variable amounts of oxygen are absorbed by the stomach and intestines during digestive processes. "Passed gas" of this composition is enough to suppress fire by oxygen denial. Researchers at the University of Virginia's Sandridge-Casteen Institute, having subjects

drink a .25 liter mixture of equal parts club soda, pineapple juice and goat's milk, have succeed both in increasing the proportion of nitrogen (to 38% or +8) and on-average-released volumes to 30 cubic centimeters, an increase of 18% over control. At these levels, the expelled gasses can suffocate a small waste paper fire in seven seconds (standard deviation). Problems of aim and posterior protection from heat effects remain. The National Safety Council and Underwriters' Laboratory guidelines have not changed and are clear: never attempt to extinguish a fire (of any size) with flatulence. (Inflammatory hazards represented by the presence of trace amounts of hydrogen sulfide are addressed in auxiliary memorandum, SandCast EP566B)

Why is the 21ˢᵗ century the greatest era for art?

Because in this time of unlimited aesthetic potential, depravity and poverty (total self-indulgence being extreme poverty), we can best appreciate the constrained magnificence of the past. Monteverdi's *Orfeo* was never so beautiful debuted in the court of Mantua by a cold choir of boys, as now. [Editor's note. Cf. Nietzsche, MA, 223.] The crucial element in creativity is resistance, opposition to tyranny, social control, physical and psychological limitation. It fuels the f(l)ight. "Everything is possible" and "anything can be said" pools into self-indulgence where the psyche in question is not the creative one in its conflicts compelled to resolution and artistic self-forgetting but everyday Joe Ego in all his anxious triviality.

What is to be done?

Nothing. The most ethical action is inaction, a position that short circuits the charged, complex network of good and evil acts.

I am a person looking for a path and have not found it. I do not have a guru or he has not yet endowed me with my most secret mantra. What should I do?

There is no harm in meditating on a default mantra, the most profound ever generated by the West. Commit to memory:

"Love suffereth long, and is kind; love envieth not; Love vaunteth not itself, is not puffed up, doth not behave itself unseemly, seeketh not her own, is not easily provoked, thinketh no evil; rejoiceth not in

iniquity, but in truth; beareth all things, believeth all things, hopeth all things, endureth all things. Love never faileth: but where there be prophecies, they shall fail; where there be tongues, they shall cease; whether there be knowledge, it shall vanish away. For we know in part, and we prophesy in part. But when that which is perfect is come, then that which is in part shall be done away. When I was a child, I spake as a child, I understood as a child, I thought as a child: when I became a man or a woman, I put away childish things. For now we see through a glass, darkly; but then face to face: now I know in part; but then shall I know even as also I am known. Faith, hope, love, these three abideth; but the greatest of these is love."

Love always has an object. In this mediation, the first focus should be on one's friends and loved ones; next acquaintances and strangers, lastly enemies. When one can at least conceive of those hated as potential objects of love, the practice may broaden out to include all sentient beings, excluding mosquitoes, viruses and various parasites. Not to be preachy; most folks do prefer method to transcendence. [Editor's note: 1 Corinthians, 13, 4-13. Nelson has conflated elements of the Tyndale and KJV versions, with minor alterations.]

What was the most gracious act in human history?
Impossible to say if by history we mean all that has occurred since most of what is done is never chronicled. If we mean upon record, exempting such deeds of commendation as kidney and lifeboat seat donation, or what was commonplace, pilots staying at the yoke of the flaming plane so that their crews might bailout, our answer requiring a kind of stylistic finish, then one act surpasses all others: that Marie Antoinette, sick, bereft of husband and children, brutalized over many months, tied up in an open cart for the slow trip through the howling mob to the guillotine, standing on the platform surrounded by a sea of hateful faces, could say after stepping on the executioner's foot, "Excuse me, Sir. I did not mean to do it."

[*A Guide to the Perplexed* is continued on page 104.]

Author's Preface

It won't matter much when all that remains of your grand passions (what you thought was most real about you) is specks of dust in the deep cup of a decayed, discolored brain pan. Which is not to say people might not visit your resting place and revelrize a generalized pathos over your grave. It happens everyday. Cremation, on the other hand, equals annihilation; no one invests much imagination in a urn, however well wrought, of undifferentiated dust gathering same in the garage, basement or columbarium that often is for economy's or the environment's sake, high sand content concrete powder. No one is going to care that you lived and died or take time to peruse your catalogue of griefs and that is as it should be. Only one thing preserves, transforms, makes them real, pitiable – writing (monuments being a kind of symbolic script). A library is the nearest thing to the mind of god.

The postmodernist project having successfully modeled despite its hostility to "types", the de-centering of the subject as evidenced by the deconstructions of Derrida and Deleuze, I say, rather they say, the destruction of "character" rendering less than plausibly plausible the fantasies of traditional narrative (Simon says), not to mention the physical effects, rather defects of the quantum, the thousands of makers will still spend their times wailing weaving resisting healthy recreations of all kinds, therapeutic and prophylactic, golf, volleyball, hiking, croquet, fencing, vaulting, tennis, table tennis, bowling, regulated boxing, leapfrog spring summer and winter, events in every Sophoclean element; foot and car racing, in boats, upon ski; horse, dog and pigeon varieties, political and marble, racing of all kinds over hill and down dale recorded at the intersection of yards, meters and any calibrations temporal, continuing, despite the tennis, to fabricate, as valiorumized by Wimbledon and Dobbs (who briefly knew Foucault) the story, "histoire" in the French sense of dressing, caps and coiffured mutts, start and stop racing the usual stuff and enough of that not to mention the tennis, concrete, clay and grass.

In your hand then, a *history* no more compelling, less perhaps, than the recorded exploits of General Brassidas Bone at the Battle of Mount Joy des Almonds (1812, The Iberian Campaign). Our motto: Read on, March on! Caveat lector; here lies no plot of fiction, grave or light. If you desire a novel's diversions, its fantasies of character and action, scan any or all of the thirty exquisitely crafted three hundred plus paged novels written each year in English by masterful young writers and published by reputable houses (Gerber and Guber).* Better yet, "settle" for the universal corpus of Dickens, or George Elliott (and I bet you won't even if you are a tenured professor on the locust cycle of every seventh year off.)

On offer, a *history*, an indulgent one of no interest to anyone now or in the most probable of predicted futures with its multitudes negotiating the congested maze of Sao Paulo, Lagos or the District Federal, sweating in the struggle for life with no need of these delicate episodes of rueful triste, pastel vignettes of despised love depicting the truth, the sooth, the nothing extenuated moot. [Editor's note. Cf. Othello, V:ii.341.]

(What is it that Mosley says? "The point of demonstration is not the creation of illusion but explanation of an occurrence." Did we say that already? Fine, we have just begun to rant.)

*Full disclosure. I had, in fact, submitted this manuscript to the distinguished publishing house Fubar and Fubar; it was rejected. Only after considerable insistence did they share with me a part of their (anonymous) reader's negative report; I quote: "Writing should always advertise a victory, an overcoming of oneself which needs to be communicated for the benefit of others. This dyspeptic author hasn't digested his bitter morsel and is trying to transfer his sourness as a compensatory exercise of power, seeking victory over a victimized reader that he has failed to achieve or even attempted over himself." To which I can only reply that such an over masticated repudiation does indicate a victory over somebody, namely this publisher's all too human dog's body, an aka Junior Lecturer (English) type at Sydney Sussex Poly in North Scrimshaw, only two hours away by train, let's say, from F & F's headquarters in lower Hempstead where the ferny folk live.

Actually, I'm not a not nice person but a proud one, which probably makes it worse.

For whom?

Dad

The old man is leaving his younger wife in bed to take a walk and have some quality time with his little son. Full disclosure. I'm that lad and I'd like to ask "Dad, hadn't you bonked enough?" Back story. It would have been a hot August night six years earlier in the stifling Norfolk Virginia tenements, rasping cicadas plastered against the screens, and it makes sense kinda, cooling down by getting hotter. My mother-to-be figures an old man won't be up to much. He figures a forty-five year old woman isn't fertile and really, why should a septuagenarian with an exceptional boner have to settle for the insulated sensation of an industrially thick Cold War condom, an ounce of prevention prevented that nine months later led to me and my latter day inquiries.

Dad wasn't mean or cold, just distant. He read *The Daily Pilot* and *The Evening Star*, he loaded bitumemous stacks of clacking 78s on a boxy Victrola (manufactured ca. 1920, with its label of the listening white dog, cherished memento of his younger maturity), and turned the tarnished brass crank; he paced around, sprinkling roach powder (genuine pre-Carlson DDT) along the gaping molding, fussed with an accordion-trunked camera on a rickety tripod standing like a big weird bird in the living room that never, ever worked. He'd leave our three room apartment on Sunday afternoon to catch the bus to catch the ferry to catch the bus on Monday that would take him to his job as a parts clerk at Langley USAF base, Hampton. On Friday, he reversed the route back to us in Norfolk.

Okay dad, another question: why do you spend 80% of the week self-exiled from the constancy of your little family's creche? Maybe in your self-absorbed way you preferred the anonymity, your Hampton boardinghouse's dry isolation. Maybe you had a girlfriend. Having raised two daughters from your first marriage (wife deceased), maybe parenting holds no charm for you. Maybe you're simply tired, po(o)ped out.

We got along just fine; he didn't bother me, I didn't bother him. I was mama's boy, all that mattered. So even as a five-year old, I noted the novelty, grabbing my red spongy ball, when he said we were going out for a walk to the local park.

There, I played my favorite game of tossing it high and catching it or even more fun, missing it so it would bounce over my head for a panting second chance. As I ran around, a temporary child under a falling ball, his gaze followed me over the living green clearing. In eight months, he'd be dead. He must have just gotten the diagnosis, though in those days they'd have to cut him up to be sure ("exploratory surgery", too optimistic a phrase) – stomach cancer. He sat there, knowing he was going to die and leave his kid to the care of a lethargic fifth grade educated woman with thyroid disease whose only income would be his fourteen years of low level service government pension. Not a good feeling, I bet.

Here's another interrogatory: why after a lifetime of work, your adulthood riding the rising fortunes of these United States (and you, a literate white man in Jim Crow's Virginia) and not attestably a drinker or gambler or spendthrift, why did you gather no moss so that when you finally retired and moved in with us that last year in Norfolk, the sum of your inheritable property was two tired cow hide (grain like stain) suite cases of clothes, the Victor-Victrola talking box and the sad camera with the drooping snout?

This would be a question I'd put later to my mother (whom adversity had made oddly gentle) who said with rare and out of character fervor, "his mean old daughters took everything." They lived in nearby Newport News and never visited except to attend his funeral, contributing nothing to its cost or a marker. I don't remember much about them – they were tall (everybody was) and wore black (everybody did). What's the reason, Jack? (Incest, a bitter adultery, disputed property, hatred of his remarriage?) I'm left with a watchful old man on a bench, thinking, "I've got two grown daughters that despise me and an accidental son I'm leaving in poverty. That's my legacy." So many mysteries in a life, so many unspoken sorrows (and let's not forget, unspoken joys).

Dad, I turned out alright; there was welfare and scholarships and I wasn't drafted to Vietnam. One thing I was determined to do. I would tell my sorrows and expose my mysteries to insure they didn't disappear like yours into the black hole of undifferentiated pain. My epithet not "suffered in silence" but "a trace in language." (And dad, I'm not even sure you really existed, since apart from that walk, you're dim and distant. But somebody pistoned me into existence one hot night, August 1951 and I grant you were *an influence*.) [Alternate self-epithets: "He passed gas in language." "He gassed the past in language." "He surpassed his dad in language."]

Playing different Games, they are playing the same
(Old Dutch proverb)

They are both too knowing even the sly dog which we assume is his but might be hers (professional women have been known to employ guardian canines) a card counter hound perhaps, communicating by wags of tail. In a room, in the night, the man and woman are playing Seduction, which Baudrillard, the sharp eyed identifier of killer squirrels (see his *American Diary*) calls the most human element in sex. (Presumptively animals cannot seduce. Having observed squirrel behavior, their touching embraces in what they took to be the privacy of their high limbed tress, I'm not so sure.) The enshadowed chamber is lit up with the radiance of attraction, genetic voltage, the attraction of ions, nanoscopic charges arcing at the synapse with every movement and motion of thought. A micro physics that provides the only rational argument for astrology – that at the smallest cellular confluence of conception, some gravitational pull, however minute, from Saturn and Jupiter might affect your-to-be developed character. If so, how greater the effect must be that your mother was reclined upon steel box springs, possessors of an even larger small attractive force, the greatest sign in your astrological chart, Sleepepedix. Indeed, I recall the squeaks and metallic squeals the night I was conceived (it is, unsurprisingly, my first memory) though whether it was the bed coils or mom or a duet, I cannot say.

I ride the subway, see my unattractive fellow man and think "we have been of woman born, our mothers have groaned for us," this a more immediate bond of brotherhood than the Buddhists' hype that Hitler was my great, great, great, great gadfather, kind and loving to me, back when we were fleas, though expounding this basis of affection will likely end with your new found frater attacking you with any weapon at hand, even his so recently placid hands.

This is all too lite when what I want is to hit the sexual depths, how in this little room, they make a reckoning, she anticipating the pride of possession and attendant pleasure and he the immediate pleasure and a subsequent possession ("Bess, you is my woman now"). Off this curtained stage, two other actors you think, the betrayed? And each she and he is self-seduced and seducing as they deploy like minor gods the game pieces on the table, tendering their feints and forays before the general advance and double envelopment. Note the phallic, enflamed candle, the open mouth of the receiving cup, her ace below the waist of hearts.

The world must be peopled. [Editor's note: Cf. *Much Ado About Nothing*, II, iii, 262]

Old, Tired and Possibly Sick, Professor Van der Mule Still has Kick

Most of my professors at Great State were donkeys in doctoral robes, like this sad ass. Dull, dim or burnt-out, wasn't he once motivated, kicking at the stall? Now at spring break, the long range of rooms (UVa!) emptied of students, might he not in white muzzled age stagger again towards the tree of his inspiration (Donne, Plato or Hegel?) that seems like himself, old, battered and yet deep rooted, taping an ever fresh and sacred fount. See – it presents young shoots with reaching leaves. His is this restoring vision and just in time; soon, groping or is that waving, he must take the path to the bridge and cross the still waters.

"I was always different, different even when very young … when all the other donkeys pranced and brayed, I did too, *with a difference*; I did because they did, my heart wasn't in it. I preferred ruminating in the hay strewn barn where I could kick the hardest, run the fastest. The world was not as if should be. There was Jenny lovely little Jenny, diminutive, she of the brightest eyes and glossiest grey-brown coat, coltish in her motions. I never had a chance with her. So many bolder, bigger Jacks. She was never haughty or unkind to me, would smile, offer a friendly nuzzle. This made her more attractive than had she been the proud conventional beauty. I could have her in my mind; a sweeter world of imagination. I discovered reading – a cosmos of all possibilities, a universe of better worlds.

Schools, the various academies, always somebody to answer to but I was good enough at criticism, takes on texts, I could see the angles, and in time (though it did not seem so timely), naturally, I was teaching, with promotion and tenure. In the larger lectures, I understood as some of my confident colleagues did not, the necessity of showmanship; you are on stage, your pupils an audience of the anonymous, all that youthful energy confined to a seat, what they must feel – resistance and boredom. Time for the old Hee Haw! My little mannerisms and entertaining quirks, a rota of jokes and rhetorical, unanswerable questions. The smaller seminars were harder. What to say? It has all been said or it required a cannier mind than mine to present convincing novelty. It was best to ask a question and listen, very, very deliberatively. "What should we make of Falstaff?" And he or she would offer "An antiquated holdover, a vice figure from morality plays." This was standard; good, they'd done the reading.

Begin with affirmation. "Yes, I agree." Then ask – "Who else in the play is architypised (a vile term that gets their jargon-hungry attention)? The aptly named Shallow? Hotspur? If they are not, what problem does it make that the fat figure is on a different plane or on several planes? Is it a problem? Yes, No?" I had no great pupils but enough degree-getters to satisfy the state's quota and the years – an article every other year, rolled on.

These days I'm less at ease even in the big classes. What are those tiny phones, the flat screens they take notes on (if they are)? What are they thinking, what are their lives like?

(My friend Carsen says "They are like what we were like, yearning, young." Possibly, but they look blanker, smarter.) Do I really reach them? Does Shakespeare? My deferential assistants do the grading.

My life has been good; bachelor donkeys know how to kick up their heels at conventions. No gelding, I've had my smiling successes in the vast evenings in the strange city after the last presentation or panel, my long face bordered by bright bottles in the bar's mirror, the seat beside me vacates and is filled, my glass empties and is filled. Spirits rise. "Hello."

Soon, it will all end. Not, I bray, too soon. I will pass over the bridge into the deep wood. I have been to the verge in my dreams and heard Jenny laughing.

Young Devils

Another old geezer, past all pleasure except drink and even that's become a tasteless habituation. Tending his needs (and the catatonic, imbecile dog's) is no job for a cocky apprentice imp. When big Mister Red gave us our assignments he said Earth was a great opportunity, get in on the ground floor. Hee hee hee. Hell, it's like working at McDonald's, no scope and fiendishly boring. The world is full of troublemakers already. Still, there's an outside the window that's spacious and the painting suggests there's always some hot young couple that would enjoy a loving cup of bedevilment. The old guy can't last long, wheezing all day, snoring all night, licking wine from a sieve. Impossible to believe the randy-andy in the picture was him.

Stopping By Fens On A Misty Evening

A landscape of cloud-broken light over the rider's left shoulder projecting into mist, his umbraged double. Does he contemplate the roads not taken?

I would pass you on the sidewalk; we nodded. I wanted to speak and could not bear to speak. I wasn't discontented, my excellent companion, busy with her morning routines, was just there, back up the walkway, our bedroom windows looking down on where, you, the Other walked. I was happy but everyone twenty-five to thirty-five is searching and susceptible – to what? Susceptibility, the not-known, you, your fast-paced walk and dark, semi sad enigmatical beauty, lineaments inseparable from intelligence.

What I knew: I had seen your picture on the English graduate student picture board: I was drawn to it just striding by, the lustrous one inch by one inch icon of a photograph. Then the syllabus where your name jumped out – The Early Novels of Henry James. You must be post-Masters to teach that course! Easy for me, even as a worker (with a dual major in History and Eng Lit) to get permission to take it. But among the undergrads, wouldn't it have been all too obvious what the object of my study was? Which realization should have been one way or another, the end of it. What was the point in attempting failure and even more hazardously, success? I was happy, remember?

Except, weeks later, I saw you, laughing (a revelation, a New Found Land), luminous on the arm of my friend, acquaintance, actually, [...] [Editor's note: the author has left a space for a proper name, never supplied.] the English Department's great white hope (hype) at the ABD level. Whom I had met one weekend when my companion was out of town and I went to a bar, lonely not looking, sat beside him and we talked – New Criticism, Postmodernism, baseball, you name it. I did most of the listening.

When next we met after seeing him with her, for by now we were on terms, I played my third beer gambit "So who is that pretty woman I've seen you with?"

"Oh, that's Vera, Veraaaa Fielder, I guess we're an item." He drew her name out, possessively, ending with a big toothy equine grin, rare from him. "Congrats!" I made a motion to clink his glass in total sincerity since they were magnificent together, an Alpha-coupling.

Weeks later, I learned from one of his disciples, (yes, once he was on my radar screen I saw how other male students copied his mannerisms, the flare of success, his occasional out thrust hand, the arched, mid-discourse brow, the tilted back, wryly attentive head, the skeptical up twist of lip) he was gone, PhD done, defended. Job offered, taken at Western State, "Vera, do you know her, went out with him. She'll finish her PhD out there." Valid report. End of story.

Yet not a month, not a week I didn't think of you, of him. He deserved you and this justice in a world where justice is very hit or miss, obsessed me. Why should anything be so right? Thanks to the developing world wide web, I could look you up, see that you and him for six years shared the same blue skied address. The same bed. Then for ten years, you couldn't be found. Meaning what? One day upon a random search, a break from my tedious job, you surfaced, teaching freshman composition at "City College" 500 miles form tenure-docked […], living with (a reverse telephone number check) – The Exxon Mobile Professor of Geophysics at Stanford!, married, retaining your maiden name. So you had done well, matched with a properly statused prof who as evidenced by his posted photo from a mountain hike was a natural Mister Natural, a good guy sporting a flannel shirt, backpack and husband material smile. Though there's no sign you'd ever gotten your PhD. The void in your resume was the usual children (see *his* proud papa-on-website-resume).

It all made sense. […] was too intense, too self focused (and almost certainly still too successful with women) to last when what you wanted, you hardly knew: a home, a garden, a family. So, after recriminations and tears, the long nights when it seems dawn will never come, you have made your good, decent life. Me too, with the same more than compatible companion. The one, did I say, who looks rather like you.

If I had stopped you on the street, followed up hello, said "Can we talk? I know this is crazy but ..." and with kindness and curiosity, you had assented, what then? The rider looks at his shadow self. Did he have her, does she have her own shadowed self?

As it is, you have never given me a thought in these ten thousand days. What we are we sometimes think we know, what we might have been, we cannot see. Does any of this matter to anyone? Yes, to one man who isn't.

Author's Abstract

This is the border crossing. Gray Grenzland, shifting liminal light. Time to turn back. Ahead, banal, commonplace terrain, (ah, madam it is common) populated by four figures, Karen, Dennis, Janet and Guy in the usual three planes of time.

Past. Karen and Dennis were married as undergraduates. They are friends with a fellow student, Guy.

After graduation, Karen attends graduate school full time in European history; Dennis gets a job in the library.

"Present". (Pay attention.) The marriage has dissolved after three years because of Dennis's involvement with an hourly wage worker at the library, Janet, a dissertation student in Classics. She is already acquainted with Karen who following the breakup with Dennis has become intimate with Guy. The two new couples, Guy/Karen, Dennis/Janet, after a year's adjustments in the new relationships are constant companions, going out together, meeting at each others separate abodes, taking trips to the nearby big cities, Richmond and Washington, best friends. The relationships are not "open", Guy wants from Karen some kind of commitment which she will not give, while Dennis and Janet have tenders (vows and how), explicit understandings of loyalty and exclusiveness. All move on a lava field of unresolved issues, fire below the surface.

Now it so happens that on Sept 22, Karen is out of town visiting her mother for the weekend. Dennis, writing a novel, has told Janet he needs to be alone the same weekend to make progress on the masterpiece he feels he has been neglecting. These interruptions have been the cause of some disagreement between them. He says they are no different from the time she must devote to study, she says those are regular and predictable, his are not, and he is always the one deciding their time.

Missing Karen, Guy feels lonely and drives to over to see his old chum Dennis who doesn't open the door. He drives over to Janet's assuming Dennis is, as he frequently is to the aforesaid neglect of his novel, there. What happened next is … all so incredibly pre-portable phone. A "Handi" (German for mobile phone) would have been handy. For want of an Apple, we are condemned to this fall (in German, "Fall" meaning "case") of wo/man.

Fore worded is forewarned. The border gate rises portentously. Ahead, detours, switchbacks, twists into future, stops in the action, speed traps, the unendurable moment. The skies change everyday.

Guy's finger, paint tainted at the tip, lightly taps on Janet's door.

How to Win Friends and Influence People
(Dennis's First Recollection)

It can't be said my friend was attractive, being curtailed of fair proportion, what with the truculent face of an aged baby, lank wisps
of urea-blonde hair, a hooked nose, sloped shoulders gulching a
caved-in chest over a protuberant belly burdening a limp so that
when he walked he swayed, the entire effect slightly, significantly
hideous, giving cause for passing wonderment (and barking dogs):
a failed human-alien union, an alcohol foisted fetus, an undigested
dough boy, an unlicked albino bear's whelp, a catastrophic genetic
mash-up half Loki, half Gollum? How was such a figure my friend?
Accident, pure accident. Call it luck or life, an intersection of time
and space … Fate.

　　See — there he is, ugly enough to generate the pull of pathos
which is a kind of allure, a solitary figure lurching down the sidewalk, a bent particle in a college town's fall physics: under clear
skies and seventy degrees, the stadium's strong attractor making of
the surrounding streets a vacancy distantly disturbed by the crowd's
rippling roar and the score-report, the Home cannon firing.

Karen and I were coming back from the A&P, "Home" games being a good time to shop, the store beckoning with various pre-game specials, good deals on beer, chips, frozen pizzas, meats of all kind, nobody in the checkout docks to distract the chatting clerks. Even with grocery bags in each hand, we were faster than the Gimp, not that passing would be a quick. Ample time for Karen to make one of her focused studies.

"Isn't he a classmate?"

"Kinda. He was in my philosophy intro, the guy who insisted on being called "No Man". Carsen was cool about it... "Now Mr. No Man, would you say the proposition 'The King of France is wise' is true or false?" Karen, who had already taken Carsen's Advanced Logic and gotten an A, had no further interest in putative Kings of France. She observed "Paint stains on his shirt. He's an artist." It was she who as we came abreast asked "Is your name really No Man?" Me, I had no need whatsoever of freakish-artistic friends. But the friendship began right there as we walked beside the almost traffic free Route 29. How easily we talked, ambling pleasantly three abreast alongside the temporary ribbon of concrete park. He invited us over to his place that evening for wine (he drank *wine?*) and chamber music. I wasn't sorry, both were better than I'd ever experienced, a Schist noir, a Schubert quartet. We were into art and culture and began to see a lot of each other. When Karen was with me, he was pretty normal if usually trying too hard to be funny (admittedly, his "Reagan as talking turd" was ever various and hilarious). When in my role as male buddy, I visited him separately in his just off campus, "garden apartment" lair, with paintings all over, columns of carefully folded newspapers ("my *Washington Post* posts") rising toward the ceiling, it was different.

There, he would really switch on his antics. Once, during one of our aesthetical debates (Picasso[him] versus Matisse [me]), he suddenly went to all fours, panted and barked "Barf Barf" with an animal-in-heat swish of ass. He explained, (still on hands and knees) that whenever I saw the word "art" or "artist", I should mentally supply and if need be vocalize "barf" and "barfists". Proud of his possession of culture, he was contemptuous of all culture, even painting, his chosen medium. In his view, most artists were hopeless Daubists, excepting Leonardo, Cezanne, and Gorky. These, he allowed, might be respected, not as genius predecessors but as epigonic forerunners who viewed (or "projected", a favorite word of his) on the plane of Eternity (where art was timeless)-were in true order of precedence, HIS students. It was crazy, manically conceited; it made me laugh.

His own paintings hung amid the museum reproductions were striking – great blotches, clouds, billows of carefully nuanced color, superimposed, saturating, seeping out of the canvas, miasmic loam for vast, weirdly suggestive architectures of no known kind, Monet's water lilies engulfing Bosch's sci-fi skyscrapers and burning ghettos. Not that I was jealous; I had a wife.

He was a studious conspiracist-theorist. He had down all the angles of Dealey Plaza and the sequence of shots timed by frames of Zapruder. Did I know that presented with photos of anonymized mock-ups, no reputable forensic pathologist thought Zapruder 576 showed a bullet from the back? Had I seen the photo of five so called hobos arrested in the railway cutting behind the grassy knoll who looked nothing like real bums, one of whom was CIA operative E. Howard Hunt? Was I aware that Sirhan-Sirhan's gun only held six rounds but eight bullet holes were found in the hotel kitchen where Robert Kennedy was killed? Did I know that reputable witnesses placed James Earl Ray ten miles outside of Memphis when they gunned down MLK? I didn't know that? I didn't know much, did I?

Our big disagreement was over the Big Jew. The Big Jew, don't you know, ruled Wall Street, Hollywood, and through the Rothschilds, Europe and banking. The little Big Jews ran law, medicine, corporations and the academy. Hitler wasn't all bad, defending beleaguered blonde DNA and Northern Art against the oriental onslaught; hadn't I heard of the outrages perpetrated against German maidenhood in dental chairs all over the Reich? Hitler, a tormented because minor artist type of no talent whatsoever, was *too* humane; the "missing" Jews of Europe had escaped to America and to Israel, which now wagged the goyish dog. Only, just as I flushed at another of his "let me finish" parries and our disagreement was reaching breaking point, he'd sigh, shrug and say ...

"Please. Just forget it! Politics! What do we really know? Do have another glass of wine and I'll project some slides." (Honestly, I didn't believe him. It was a shtick, an antic, his egoistical contrariness manifesting the most banal and preposterous prejudice in order to convince by its amplitude of perverse motifs. It was posturing to mask, to defend, to compensate ... he couldn't be serious. And neither, according to him, was Hitler.) Having cued the LP, he'd load the carousel, hit the lights, flash the paintings up, discoursing knowledgably, charmingly on perspective, composition and color to the low volume background of Mozart or Bach. My impulse to grab him by the collar and give him a good shake in the name of Anne Frank receded in the glow of friendship, gratitude and another glass of wine. Karen, then still my wife, was half-Jewish and to her he was ever the soul of courtesy which, sadly, was more than could be said of yours truly.

(Oh, his real name. Guy Maximilian Mantis. "Max" Mantis (sounding like a dietary supplement or comic book villain) was hardly viable. For all practical purposes, he was stuck with "Guy". No wonder "No Man" was a temptation if not a self-recognition.)

Dennis is Menaced

Unmistakable even at this odd perspective, with his board straight shoulders, tapering torso, perfectly hemispherical hams and dreadly dreads, was All ACC and Heisman nominee, 4.2 yards per carry on the force of 210 pounds of scholarship sponsored aggression and testosteronic overflow, Rafer Sampson. Rafer (actually a nice guy) was engaged in what seemed a very drawn out tackle, grasping for a ball by no means dead. He was, to mix our sports metaphors, securely past first base, headed for a slide into Home with his teammate-opponent in this full body contact-sport none other than Janet, that svelte dark haired enigma, my student employee in the library for six hours a week, she MA, MA, all but Phd.

A space had been cleared around them, people talking, drinking, only a few watching the midfield action evidentially of some duration, chairs and a sofa pushed to the side. The smoke and pounding music was making my head ache. I needed to sit down. A boney, nicotine saturated grad student with a sour look I almost recognized, leaned towards me with her puckered, knowing smile. "It's an act, nothing will happen. She's an easy-tease." It was not a familiar phrase; I half nodded. Just then, Janet's white hand emerged from the dark cascade of locks, shifted them to one side, grabbing Rafer's tree trunk neck as if in ardor to whisper in his delicately whorled ear. With a beats-me-grin and ability, a beautiful thing too see, Rafer detangled himself like a film run backwards, Janet bounding up gazelle-agile from thick grass, maneuvering with angles and moves Rafer surely envied. Later I saw her, listening then laughing with a group of the smart set from the English department, Rafer cutting through the crowd to join them. As a communications major, he could hold his own.

It was then I decided to have her, to try to have her. Of course, I wanted her from the first moment I had seen her reporting for work in September. Who wouldn't, alerted to her long limbed, elegant movement, the dark hair dancing on her shoulders, her eyes grey green, green grey in the variant light, her look, serious, sad, seeking. Granted, I was married and I took my vow to Karen seriously. It was the most adult thing I'd ever done to make it; it was me and essential. But seeing Janet like that (I don't think she saw me though later she said she had and that was why she broke off with Rafer), being free with her herself, shameless in the middle of the floor, on display, on offer and then refusing, maybe it was the act of her refusal that made her most desirable and threw my switch of volition. Something told me the whole scene was an act pointed toward me to make it real. Right then I decided to pay the price with no doubt that Karen and my pride in my vow was the price. That's what I could bring to Janet. "I am nothing. This is what I am willing to pay." Who was I to say she wouldn't respond to the compliment and commitment. If a man leaving his wife for you wasn't commitment, what was? Sure, there were others that could do that, Prof. Carsen, the mellowing middle-aged men in her own subject. They hadn't, yet. Perhaps they had too much to lose. This was my chance. Not exactly tonight, not at this loud, ridiculous party where she clearly had her own agendas. Walking home, the decision to leave turned out a vindication because just as I'd had made it, the woman graduate student whose name I couldn't recall put her cigarette free hand on my knee, pushed her face close (and I thought "Picasso" because the planes weren't right between her hard eyes) and with a smile now of beauty pageant radiance, said "I know a woman, a real woman who could like you very much – except for one little thing." Wasn't I gratified to have the opportunity to be the perfect gentleman, confident her caveat was my beard, replying lightly "Do tell?" Outside later, I could still feel the pinch of her claw as it took me overlong, a second, to process her hissed answer "everything about you."

The irony was that Karen should have been at the party with me but had decided at the last hour not to come. She was moody that way, looking forward to something and then pulling back lest she be disappointed; her disappointments were severe. Which was fine because by that time, along with our apartment together, I had a tiny place with a bed and a desk at the top of a dilapidated former frat house that let rooms, ("Transients *Welcome*") to students, to travelers, male relatives, pale hillbillies visiting patients at the medical centre, to anyone but overnight drunks. Mine was at the top of the stairs, a former storage room adjacent to the attic proper, no windows or air except for what came from under the two inch gap between floor and door, a total fire trap with yellowish pine board siding, a floor away from the communal men's rooms and so hot in summer the silverfish took a vacation. It was something I could afford and better, in its astringency, a place for concentration, my "study" when I needed absolute solitude to write even if I put more time into practicing solitude than writing. Karen was very understanding generally, having work of her own and in this instance in particular when I said I'd go without her and retire to the study after. You see, there was absolute trust between us, which was good. Because I needed time to think. Tomorrow was one of Janet's days to work. The party was still going strong, I could hear it venting half a block away. But I'd never known her not to report for duty. [Editor's note: an account of Dennis's courtship of Janet is recorded in his novel; see *Going in Circles*, pp. 38-]

Karen as Oracle

If anybody could figure it all out-it would be Karen. Consider the strange fact that as child with an off the charts IQ, she'd been tracked, yes tracked by the government her entire life (Long story. Later). By now, she knew all three of them, in the biblical sense. She'd been married to Dennis while in college and when that was over her first year of grad school, she'd taken up with their friend Guy. That wasn't quite over. Between the men (because there had been something a little too easy about the start up with Guy, how Dennis seemed, everyone staying friends, pleased as if he had achieved a diplomatic handover or a trade that let him off the hook), there'd been Janet, the narrow bridge of her, a brief physical relationship that satisfied her intimate curiosity about the woman who had destroyed her marriage and which led, in time, to other women. Whom, she learned, she preferred. They were multi-dimensionally passionate and attuned to the essential rhythms, were softer and smelt better. Yes, she liked their taste.

She could thank Janet for that, her first taste. No awkward matter of fitting. Dennis's cock really was too big for comfort. Her comfort, anyway.

Their sex had never been good or frequent. He hurt her at the time and later, burning her with cystitis. The pills took care of that. There was no pill for his anger. He didn't strike her often and when he did, he was careful to do it on her upper arm or leg where the bruise wouldn't show. He was reliably sorry after. She shuddered. Funny, she thought, that happiness should be contingent upon fits and tolerances. Well, we're machines.

It was Saturday, late morning and she was in bed alone. Outside bright tight light, bird chirp. Yet already the air was heavy, the sun bearing down, drawing the moisture up like work, with quick shutterings, lustrous then dark from the building clouds. By 4 PM, there'd be a brimming stillness before the first distant rumble, the intense, torrential rains. It was then she missed Dennis most, someone long familiar to talk to. They'd hold hands at the window, feel the pinpricks of rain, clutch with each flash of lighting. Now she hugged her stuffed animal, a sad eyed turtle with an incongruously hopeful and goofy grin. It had a history. They had found it on a sidewalk by the dorms on student move out day, forlorn, pathetic because it was cheerful. It was closest thing to their child.

Some things were clear – she mustn't forget her tea cooling on the table beside her. He wasn't coming back, the old life was over. That she could face. Mostly, she didn't want him back. It would never work, he envied her intelligence; every good idea he took as a personal defeat, it made him sullen. Harder than their lost present, she could barely think about it, was their aborted future, things they had discussed in compensatory harmony and planned to do: the year abroad in England, the trip to the small towns of Virginia's Eastern Shore, the houses they were going to buy, the cats they were going to adopt, an exact prospective inventory of them – a grey tabby, a red tabby, a talkative Siamese. Their next trip, their annual "pilgrimage" back to National Cathedral. Here her heart clutched and her face got hot. They had gone up the first time soon after dating, a long train ride through the green tunnel of the Virginia cuttings. They were doing research for a term paper, "The Gothic Style." In the cathedral they fluttered about, noting the linkages and vault types, the long vistas of the nave. They drifted into a side chapel, deserted and so for them fragile as moths beneath stone. Suddenly grave, he took her hand and said, "I love you. I love you more than my life. Marry me." Even in the bad times, she had felt the force of that pledge and to give him credit, he did too. Until the day he said, not meeting her eyes "I'm sorry but you need to know. I'm seeing Janet Nielson." She couldn't make sense of the words, repeating "You're seeing Janet?" even as she held, like sudden broken pieces, two visions of Janet – her graduate student friend, and a menacing dark haired woman with power over her life, both suddenly strange and cutting.

They were all still friends, a curious, almost natural thing. People that knew them would stare at them together, four pistons of an improbable engine. She could see the energy. She and Dennis were over. She even now was breaking the flow with Guy. He was amusing oh yes … and nasty. Damaged so deep that the injury was his identity. Dennis and Janet – apparently smoothly reciprocating and lubricated. She gave a little snort. More was going on, an excess generated without apparent outlet. Guy and Janet. That's where the flow, the surplus was headed. She could see it now in bed as already she'd seen in when they were together, the way Janet laughed at Guy's jokes and caught herself, angling a look, an allure that sitting across from her with Guy, Karen could see – call it what, an option, just a very slight over investment of interest, attention that Janet knew she could, should show openly rather than make something of it by suppression. It was there and Dennis, beside her, didn't get it. Karen could feel sorry for him but it wasn't for her to tell him. Not now, after all that had happened. It was something inevitable, like physics, like the fit of stone. It would have to work itself out. Without thinking, she pushed the turtle under her pillow.

Going in Circles is a Kind of Drilling

Dennis was at a sticky point in his alchemically themed novel. He was having trouble fully envisioning, fleshing out the conjunctio of Mercury and Venus, whose metallic anagrams were mercury and soft, adulterated gold. It was going nowhere.

His concept was four characters, compounds of nature and nurture that would through interaction and experience be transformed, transmuted, refined, embodying the four seasons, the four elements, temperaments, the quadra-qualia (hot, cold, moist, dry) and cardinal directions, ornamented by the four noble truths, the four modalities of life and art: start, stop, increase, decrease, the four fundamentals of finance (earn, spend, invest, borrow), the four Fs (Fate, Fight, Flight, Fuck) and the four food groups. Life as narrative, like quick silver, fluked and flowed around his narrow corrals. He resigned himself to writing a reasonably normal narrative, a template whose essential critical mass he'd centrifuge (via the strain of extensive revision) to objectify his denser design. Did not his admired Virginia Woolf totally revise, at exhausting cost, her novels four times? Couldn't he if need be rewrite a mere twice? Hadn't the entire Tennessee Valley been harnessed to produce a mere thirty pounds of U235? He was distracted. There was a lot of traffic along his brain cock continuum.

Granted, he wasn't making it easy for Janet but working herself at lofty levels of classical tragedy, he knew she understood the sacrifice; it had to be this way. It was hard, no art would come from being on top of her, unless that was a kind art. What was that Shakespeare quote, from A Winter's Tale... "Over that art which you say adds to nature is an art that nature makes ...?" He stared into space. Time for another Rheingold.

[Editors' note: To preserve the character of Dennis' manuscript as a work in progress, it is presented without editorial emendation.]

Capt'n Jack, clad in his usual uniform of soiled tartan pants (anciently, Clan Macgregor) and frayed tweed jacket (today a dim slim green, a Brook Bros gray that had become so) and VFW forage hat that had seen hard service, was just standing there, his elaborately liver spotted hands folded over his open fly in posture of patience and meditation, the very picture of a kind of wooden Indian dignity except for his mouth moving mechanically as if trying to expel its last blue tooth. It was, as Adrian knew, just a re-charging hiatus, that in a moment he'd let loose with non-stop narrative on one of his habitual themes. Hopefully his Xeroxes would be done by then. The hood of the machine was up and Adrian was using one of his specialized tools, a bent paperclip to free the last pressure bound clot of jammed paper, the last of Capt'n's request from yesterday, "research materials" from the rare books department, copy requests out of family histories that were only restricted to prevent maenadic blue haired matrons, in their genealogical frenzies, from ripping them off from open stacks. The morning murmur in the nearby check-in-lobby and reading room was picking up. But in the Special Collections Photo-lab, a fancy name for a dusty alcove and a road weary Xerox machine, all was quiet as Adrian grim-grimaced at an odd angle, struggling, then freeing the jam.

"All clear, Capt'n."

"Very good Mr Nelson. Have you my book on the James River Settlements there?"

"Yes Sir". "

"Now the Nelsons as you may know are one of the great landed Virginia families,come-over the first one about 1630 to the York peninsular and mostly stayed except for that Bucks County branch. Thomas Nelson, the Signer, the most prominent and the rest gentry farmers, professionals, lawyers and doctors, none of them laggardly, you must know in the war of Independence or in, as some call it, the second either though in Virginia it was a close call affair, as you know, whether to leave the Union or no..." He paused and Adrian knew that both for politeness and to re-set the Capt'n's motor he should say "Yes Sir." They moved into the sepulcher lobby, the massive card catalogs consoles surmounted by bronze busts of forgotten literary worthies looking like shrunken and wind dried trophy heads. Amy the desk clerk stared with a pinched faced look. Most people didn't care for the Capt'n's seasoned odor of sweat, cheap tobacco and bourbon. Most doubted his status as a captain of any kind though Adrian knew from Walter Runk, one of his hydra head of bosses (and the only worthy), the library's memory man, that Jack had served on a landing ship off Okinawa "Army rank, not navy. "He was odd, two year ahead of me here at Virginia. Everybody knew him. Always tuned to a different drummer and so forth. But he became" and Runk, always a gentleman pursed his lips, struggled to find the words, "rather more idiosyn-cratic after that." Still, Jack had gotten his GI Bill Masters, taught Southern History to several indistinguishable generations of coated, tied and crew cut fraternity lads "until such point as he met, ah, mid-nineteen sixties the Countess and the rest is history, Russian and American, depending."

And truth to tell Adrian found something reassuring about the Captain, a quality of authenticity if authentically what was hard to tell. Adrian tried to take his cue in this and all library matters (except administration) from the gentlemanly and memorious Runk, also in Adrian's mind the real thing if too assertively fine a dresser with his three piece suits, silk pocket handkerchief silvertie claps, watch chain, button hole and spats. It made sense. If everyone recognized Runk was a hopeless manager, everyone knew he was good at other things, like research. And Runk knew people knew and hence his dandyism that was trumpery and the hoisting of a flag.

And today Adrian was grateful to Runk who made the Capt'n welcome and to the Capt'n for his lulling monologue in raspy, smoke cured Virginian, talk he knew. "Tobacco made those families. And un-made them. After five harvests, the soil is good for nothing except bad tobacco. Now they say Pocahontas taught John Rolfe to throw a fish, shad I'd expect, at the root of each plant and I believe she did. Imagine trying to do that for even 5 acres, Mr Nelson; it can't be done. So you have to expand the cultivation, and then the labor to work the fields, which meant more people from Africa and I think we can see where this was headed ..."; it was sedative and this was good because it was Monday, her day to work and soon (9:30) she would be there and he would freeze up, hardly drawing a breath before the vision of her beauty and grace.

He heard the outer door slam, then saw grim Pamela Hawkins's hard heeling in at a military pace, her sharp pressed slacks, the handbag over the shoulder, and not a word of greeting to anyone, her jaw set, looking straight ahead. And then almost before he knew, her "assistant" passed, three steps behind as if attached by an invisible chain.

It had been at the beginning of summer that Hawkins had first flashed by in the stacks with a tall, lean, dark haired young woman in tow.

"This is Adrian, the stacks guy. Adrian, Janet, my assistant. She will be working on the Heinz pamphlets."

In brisk Hawkins style, they moved off. What struck him how was how Janet had never taken her eyes off the older woman, giving him a chance for a long look at her long aristocratic features, pale skin, firm, full lips and something wary, set-back in the startling sea green eyes.

————————————

That morning she had awoken in gray light and the flutter of sparrows, it seemed to her, in the lacy flounces. The room began to sort itself out in masses, shapes that still were not familiar to her even after many nights. She turned her head and saw in a corner by the bed table one of the crickets that had soothed her with its cool, constant, nothing-human-in-it chirping. She saw books on the shelves and knew before her eyes cleared to read the titles, from the color spectrums of their spines, she was not in her room, she was in the room of exile. The birds took a sudden pause in their quarrelling. It was time for Pam's breakfast. She put on her robe and walked down the short dim hall to the kitchen that with its clean nautical surfaces and expectant implements, the obliging pots, was always a comfort to her, an ontology of no reproof.

They had never teamed in the kitchen where Pam was, as in so many ways, a solo perfectionist. Here they had never quarreled. Turning on the gas was festive, how many times had she brought to bloom that blue petaled flower -- two years? Some section of 700 days? She turned and reached above the refrigerator for the ground coffee, took Pam's favorite mug off the hanger, hand fired gift from some artist friend surely lover decades ago and turning to the counter she heard the pop. The mug was in pieces on the floor from no cause she knew and still she heard the pop, the shards on the floor unrecognizable, alien, devoid of value. Inert, broken there was nothing to do except pick them up, find another cup and go through the motions of making the brew which gurgled in the coffee maker sighing as it drip, drip, dripped while she opened the bread box, dropped the slice in the toaster and waited for the hop.

She walked backed down the hall to Pam's room and knocked.

"Come in. Hello Dearie."

Pam was looking above her book, the room awash in green ivy filtered light. It was a strong beautiful face and the person it most resembled, Janet thought was Admiral Chester Nimitz. She said nothing and came up to the bedside with the tray. Pam's tight smile froze and died in her eyes.

"Where's my cup?"

"It broke."

Janet did not mean to evade responsibility but only to explain. She could still see the pieces of ceramic, scattered in a dimension that was real and wouldn't go away. Now Pam was pale with anger, rising higher in the bed, "YOU broke it! Stupid, stupid girl. Come here." Janet moved a step closer. "Tell me how stupid, stupid you are." Janet stared and did not understand. Then she did, yes, like the cup breaking. Indeed, she had been stupid not to understand. She couldn't say the words. Soon they would be getting ready for work and the drive in the small car that would be terrible with a hateful silence unless … So she lowered her head and said, her voice hardly wavering.

"I'm stupid. I'm stupid."

A coffee table, a massive Nauga hide sofa, the TV and at the four corners, live. bio-morphing larvae lights. After a time one hardly noticed the column of newspapers, neatly folded, reaching to the ceiling and another, knee high, under construction. Guy called them his diurnal clocks. Adrian just sat there, coffee in hand while Guy monologued about philosophy or most often art, prancing about the room, slide-clicker in hand, lecturing on one of his projected slides, in this case, Bosch's Garden of Earthly Delights filling the space of the opposing wall, left bare for projection. In the next room, the inner sanctum, were scores of canvases leaning against the walls, some tacked to the wall, others rolled. One could smell strongly in the warmer months the insinuating almost sweet mix of linseed oil, paint and turpentine. It seemed in this case, the odor of the Garden. The students downstairs came and went, there were no complaints.

[Lecture on the Garden follows].

Having worked himself over to the wall edge, he flicked the switch, the ceiling light came on; it was finished. Lank whips of blonde hair stuck to his forehead, Adrian could see that the underarms of his painted splattered and frayed white cotton shirt were stained. He slid the slide clicker into his pocket, then assumed the position of parade rest, feet apart, hands clasped behind his back, an incongruous posture for one so slight, not to mention the shirt tail half out. This was one of Guy's attitudes, British army (the Duce was another favorite) a kind of joke or was it? There was gravity in the pale, thin hook nosed face, the face of a pre-youth or an old man. Happily, a professional attribute, since Guy was now the library's night guard.

He'd started out in the reserve book room where his tart asides ("Not worth reading," "You'll never understand this.") to undergraduates were about to get him fired when administration finally realized that after hours the library hosted an odd nocturnal population consisting of grad students, the homeless, young lovers and fraternity probates. The massive building could apparently accommodate them all without conflict or notice until a professor (emeritus) was found one bright morning in a carrel, permanently slumped over a copy of The Anatomy of Melancholy. Action was taken, the job of night guard established and offered to Guy since as a state worker, it was far easier to transfer him than fire him. The work suited him, having the power of a clutch of keys and a police belt pendent with flashlight and walkie-talkie, patrolling, after the cops had spent a week sweeping the night people out, the voluminous reading rooms, long corridors and maze of books, alone. Still, it was hardly enough to support him, with his taste for the occasional antique or curio, expensive art books, his mechanically distressed car. Once Adrian asked him how he managed. Guy explained. "I call my mother- he lifted his fist like a handset and "tell her I'm going" and here he shrieked "TO KILL MYSELF. Money is forthcoming."

Guy gave a deep breath and left parade rest, sat on the Thonet chair beside the sofa. "Now this damsel, this sylph, this …" He looked directly at Adrian with wide hazel eyes too big for his face. "May I suggest ... the Direct Approach, very effective, I'm told. Only there's the little problem … of your current friend, bedmate, spouse, I mean your wife, dear, dearest little Karen."

"Yes, Guy." Adrian leaned forward, elbows on knees, in earnestness. "There's the problem of Karen. There wouldn't be a problem if I didn't see her at work …" Guy raised an eyebrow.

"You see Karen at work? Often? Excessive intimacy is the leading cause of matrimonial breakdown."

"No, no, I mean Janet."

Guy jumped up out of the chair and did a little Hitler dance around the room "Fuck em. Both. Fancy some Gauguin? I just got a great bunch of slides from Boston." Fine, it would be a pleasing island interlude before Guy broke out his 12 year scotch and hit Adrian up for cash.

Karen gazed at the set table, satisfied, everything was perfect. The high contrast, first firing blue willow plates, authentic and delicate, the stemmed Russian crystal, the roses in bowels of clear water, the white linen napkins with he blue trim, all the things he liked, the things they both liked and had bought together. For even though they were four months into his experiment of having rented a separate room as his study, they were still together, still in love. Perhaps that room apart took some of the pressure off, what with her needing to make progress on her dissertation and Adrian wanting to perfect his novel to apply for the writing fellowship for next year. It was sad how their writing got in each other's way when she had hoped it would be a bond between them. She had envisioned a hermitage of work and mutual support. Instead it filled all the space. He complained he could feel her working, her concentration diluted his. She would be working in the bedroom, he the living and after a time, she'd hear him pacing in the hall or opening the door to leave, as he explained later, for a walk or an errand. At a point when she wasn't ready to stop, he'd return, come in, stroke her hair and soon be after her sexually. Nor did he take agreeably to the essential manners of her life, the small things like the proper way to arrange food in the refrigerator, or clothes by season in the closets, the rituals of right order that kept her world together. And when things were bad … no, she wouldn't think of that now. His new refuge made things easier. Soon, he'd be over.

The library, until the recent erection of the steel and glass rec-plex, was the biggest building on campus, built in the 1930s as a public works

project, with a broad brick and white stucco front
conveying New Deal confidence, consonant with the
dominant campus style of pseudo Palladian. Sited on
a slope, the library presenting a low tier entrance
that expanded along its length down the hill into 8
more levels that the staff had always called decks,
that at night, the lights low or extinguished in
the near classrooms and offices, gleamed in the
dark of the hill like a ocean liner breasting a
long wave. Adrian reflected that the library had
become distorted for him, had morphed into more
than the place where he had studied as a student
and now worked. It had become an odd time-space
curvature in which he rolled around like a marble
in the plastic tracked race game of his childhood
or a pinball game. He kept going around and round
or bounced back and forth and the center he kept
gravitating back to in his thoughts was Janet.

She worked three days a week in the special
collections dept, coming in most mornings with
Hawkins and leaving at noon (as advanced grad student, her classes were in the afternoon). The days
for Adrian were strange, distorted; exhilarating
and tiring. Some auto pilot in his brain got him
through, the work was mostly routines: book fetching when students were off or on break, research
on simple reference questions, Xeroxing requests,
shifting books to make space, identifying items for
preservation, and daily, checking the shelving by
looking at the call number of books at the right
of their "flags", thin strips of cardboard, color
coded for each shelver. You could start anywhere
in the two floors of stacks as long as you finished
the inspection in a week.

Now for many weeks, where ever started, he
finished at Janet's work table in the back of the
history section, a cramped, ill-lit, lonely spot
reflecting her persona non grata status with Mrs
Brumbles, the "Director of Public Services", one
of special collections' hydra heads of monstrous

bosses. How often Adrian has seen Janet listen to one of Mrs Brumbles belligerently mumbled and incoherent directives with a pale face, standing tall, with a distant look and without a word of acknowledgment move off with a long coltish stride; she would already have been fired except no none else could do her job, inventorying the Heinz pamphlets, grey archival boxes like cinder blocks stuffed with 19th century musings on antiquity; the stuffy terminus where he would end up, pulling flags.

She was there at the end of along avenue of call number "PAs", the Greek and Latin, the deep brown spectra of calf binding and gold leaf, smelling from leather preservative and old dryness, the spine tiles gleaming in the ticky light of the flickering, bug stained florescence panels. He saw her, her dark head bent in the dim over her work, not looking up though she must have heard his heels on the industrial tiles. He had done this so many times, turning back at the last flag, not speaking to her. Today was different. He had a note.

He had realized he could not go on. He had to know if she would have him. Even that was too practical an interpretation of his state. He simply had to tell her he loved her. It might not end in rejection. Sometimes she looked up and smiled, nothing suggestive, just a recognition. Of what?

So yesterday, as a hotdog roll-boiled in the pot on the cooking coil in his basement rooms, he began to write. The expression seemed right as the words flowed. And all night, the same words as if he were speaking them that echoed in his head, he composed over and over again as if anew. By morning, he had become the words.

Dear Janet,

I love you. You are the most beautiful woman, the most beautiful being I have ever seen. Days weeks pass and I see only you. Every night, I am awake thinking, dreaming the dream of you,

the way you look, hearing the words you speak.
I don't expect you to reciprocate my feelings.
Why should you? But I had to tell you. It is
driving me crazy. I have never been felt like
this about anyone. I love you.

Writing on of his last sheets of Crane's best
bond, he got out his old fountain pen, having
bought a new bottle of dark blue ink to fill it. He
carefully cut the sheet in half. And wrote. After
it had dried, he folded it in tomorrow's shirt
pocket, over his heart.

Now a quickening in his pace that she noticed.
She seemed to see the strain in his face, no smile.
He couldn't even look at her, her beauty was unbearable. He lowered his eyes. "Here is something for
you." He extended his hand and -- a miracle — hers
took the folded square. He turned away, shaking.

The declaration, then. It wasn't unexpected. For
weeks now his awkwardness, his ability to speak to
her any longer than to convey work instructions,
most tellingly, the fact that he couldn't look her
in the face, a behavior of some of those who admired
her before (others would boldly challenge her with
a stare) and she herself had felt these things for
women. She had not wanted things to develop quite
this soon but it had happened and she needed to
think. Sol had been like that, her only male lover
so far. Third year of college, his eloquent if hyper-
verbal paeans to her beauty and grace. The puppy
dog devotion and clumsy sex until he went off to
med school and later, tho communication in a letter
that he was seeing another med student. Needless to
say, he hadn't needed to be so honest and that still
pained her. Where it did, she could respond to the
freshness in Adrian's note — the rushed words the
oh so careful handwriting with his blue half finger
print on the reverse that reminded her of being
nineteen as if the long tiresome decade in between
had never happened. OK, he was devoted, this Adrian.
In his favor: he worked hard, he had neat hands and

sincere if not very complex brown eyes. The beard was so-so. His manners were good. He was intelligent, undistinguished. Anxious. What he lacked, she knew from the two years at Columbia after Bryn Mawr where she met the big name profs and the centurions of commerce, scrubbed scented men with hundred dollar haircuts that would follower her around the Met or just sit down at her lunch table and try to pick her up. "Hi haven't I seen you before?" Or the bold asst. professor as she judged him, with a punctilious beard and a French suit who sat down and said "don't you like me?". The memory and her retort made her laugh, "Yes ... I'd like you to go away." What Adrian lacked was personal power and focus. He was ordinary and could, at any event be managed. He was married, what of that? Possibility.

The problem was Pam. Things were tangled, unresolved. She saw her, scowling, hands on hips. The angry beauty pained her. It was 1:45, time to leave for Profs Jovack's seminar on Tragedy. She quickly heeled down the long corridor of rare PRs and turned the corner, saw through the slats of metal shelving Adrian, sitting still, staring at his desk. She took a deep breath, her voice ever low and earnest called him back.

"Thank you for your note. It meant a great deal to me. I didn't expect it. I have a seminar til 5. Will you meet at the Virginian, 6:15? We can talk about this?"

He looked up, sick with emotion. "Yes, yes."

Going out the door at 5 he met Guy coming in. This happened form time to time as Guy came in early "To peruse research." Prior to his shift. They stopped at the detection gate, serenely blocking anyone that might want to pass.

"I told her".

"Told who what?"

"Told her, told her I love her." I'm meeting her in a hour."

"Ah, I'll stop by on you later." He languidly pushed through the gate.

She had been waiting there midway back in one of the place's long single line of booths, a railway effect, across from the bar with its medal ribbons of bottles, hanging "Virginia" blanket and last call bell, her white face framed by a shoulder length cascade of dark hair. He came up, she was peering ahead with a fixed gaze as if through a mask, waiting; he noticed a startling thread of silver in her hair like a glint of moonlight.

He waited for her to acknowledge him. Finally, seconds passing, she looked at him from the sides of her eyes with their northern, Baltic down hook. She lowered her head. He sat, already speaking in his head, I, I, I, but said nothing. She looked up then, her lips tightening so that the corners turned up in the slightest of smiles. He was taking her in it seemed for the first time. Had he ever looked at her before? Had he ever seen before?

A waitress appeared, He ordered a house white, same as she so as somehow not to break the spell. The bar room pop was on but they were far enough away from the black hanging spy of the speaker and cocooned by the opposing white noise of bar chat. He saw a mirror at the back, a rising curve of reflecting booth light, her black-luminous head, a mermaid, an ondine surfacing.

They walked back falling in stride down the main colligate boulevard, over planted with plane trees, he worried about being seen anxiety and yet felt authorized as all the mute familiar storefronts, the Kinkos, 7-11 and University Book Store seemed quiet, approving witnesses, a surge of confidence that crested at her place, a small apartment, Zen in its neatness and spareness, where as they passed the door, she turned and kissed him, her bed no more than 8 steps away, they tripping towards it.

She was surprised by her lubricity. She was

not interested in men, she fancied she had known men. But he was firm, his body slim and angular and urgent, all coming together in the focus of his desire. He was too fast, his kisses impossibly wet and hard, his beard distracting with tickle. She guided him in and it excited her, his excitement excited her.

"So what about your wife? You know I know her. I like her."

"I have to tell her, no way I can face and lie to her."

Guy was checking out the toilet stall graffiti, in curiously hopeful and slightly stale desperation as befitted the scrawls...

This is the two story club and bar, The Mousetrap, the first floor with wide screen sport tv, immense boom boxes emitting a loud aquarium of sound.

The upper floor, exposed beams, ferns, a lustrous copper topped bar, this the favorite watering hole of the trendy untentured profs, and grad students.

Today is Friday and the joint is really jumping, you can hear the beat and occasion cheers from downstairs.

Upstairs, our four protagonists, a table by the window. Looking at them, you'd have a hard time telling who was with who.

Perhaps surprising, given all we know, that they are there at all? Two with light hair, two dark, you might given the earnestness with which the blond woman is talking to the dark man that they are a couple and you'd be understandably wrong by a less than a year. That would leave the silent hunch backed fair man with the uncontestable beauty and the very improbability of this gives it a kind of logic. You'd be wrong there also.

Hyperlinks?

art of fugue?

[Editor's note. This document came to us claiming to be a scanned typescript, subsequently converted to WORD. The final phrases were objects of extended analysis for WRITES. As "typed", they initially present as inquiries by the character "Adrian". "Hyperlinks" however makes no sense in a document depicting the 1980s. Nor can it be it the actual author's first critical response since in a actual typescript such would have been far more likely to have been handwritten than typed. We concluded therefore, that they are second order accretions by Nelson to a possibly original typescript word processed at later date in an attempt to render the fragment less fragmentary by indication and accreditation of an absolute caesura as occurs in Bach's Art of Fugue. As such, they cannot be organically part of the character "Dennis's" novel.

I emailed Nelson for clarification and received a reply which he has not authorized for publication. It described his method of composition. He would go to bed, turn out the light as if for sleep and begin to mentally write, generally generating no more than two memorized "pages". This "text", validly inscriptional, he would word process the next morning. He complained that the transcription process was only 95% accurate as a "record of the Muse's pure channeling." After suggesting that a bedside notebook might have been useful, I asked what bearing this had on my inquiry. I received no answer or indeed any subsequent email. Nelson still maintained communication with Naomi Roth, my Personal Assistant. Of necessity then, she became the essential medium for communication with our disabled or disaffected author. Having worked directly under me, she was familiar with my strenuous personal expectations and with the established protocols of the Institute.

Crucial insights into many areas of aridity were provided by the author's friend, Guy Mantis, whom Roth described as "an inexhaustible fount of suggestibility" and by Jane Nielsen, the author's companion, who was "sympathetically if sporadically supportive." Not withstanding the exertions of the staff of WRITES, which were considerable, A Book of Emblems could only have come to fruition following their compassionately fertile irrigations.]

Ding. Janet is awarded an extra ball.

Tapping on the door.

"Hi."

"Oh, Hi, come in."

"Is Dennis around?"

"No, he's at Thompson Road all weekend …writing."

"I was just there. He didn't answer. That explains it."

Guy pauses, half turns to leave.

"Would you like to come over to my place and play some games?"("Some games" refers to Pac Man, Maze, Block Knocker, Tetris that, pre-personal computer, are accessed from a World War Two looking light-steel box made in Japan, early Atari) that plugs into the TV. Janet shows what – a little flicker in her face.

"Sure."

Because she loves the little bright screen of self obliteration when all day, at some front and back of her mind, she is dealing with Electra and Clytemnestra, with Dennis who only wants his own way and can leave her so easily after their exertions in bed. (Yes, even on non-work mornings, she would see him check his watch.) Dealing too, denying rather a shaky foundation of doubt and despair that undermines her, a dark place where scorpions sting and don't let go.

The drive over to Guy's place wasn't exceptional; she'd been in his car without Dennis several times: a trip to the dentist, delivery of her typewriter to the repair shop, a ride to the train station. The door slams and it's the usual auto intimacy, close conversational savannas opened up by uncommitted gazing ahead, body awareness in a moving metal box which may mean nothing, just being American, how we live. She had never before gone over to his place like this for a personal visit. He had never invited. So perhaps she already knew on the drive over, perhaps she had already decided.

They sit on Guy's neatly made bed, an island of square angles surrounded by the aquatic panels of his swirling murals. He watches her move the little lever that directs the game balls, tunes to her concentration and sees, not for the first time, that it diverts, defers a sadness. The room is quiet except for the minute sounds of their breaths and the game's electronic pings, metallic and miniature steel band cheerful. She has just lost a ball in Block Knocker, it gives a little sigh, kills itself by rolling off an edge. They are both utterly still, focused, faces brightened by the square of screen.

"You know, he is the one who always calls the night or weekends off. Is that fair? And has anyone, have you, ever even seen his novel? Don't say talk to him. I have. You should talk to him for me. You're an artist and you and Karen aren't like that."

Guy turns his head to her, a slight smile, bending his thin if serpents had them, lips. "No we aren't like that. She doesn't much want to see me these days, anyway. Says she may give me up entirely, can you guess (he knows she can), for women." Laughs.

Now there is that atmosphere – an aura, an electricity flow from vintage footage, dawn at Alamogordo an instant before Big Boy blows or rather the exact instance just after when a minute suffusion of radiance primes the retina or the old luminous photo of Mr and Mrs Archy Duke on the Sarajevo city hall steps, headed for the ridiculously pre-streamlined, all upholstery and accouter-mented horseless carriage that detours off the main avenue to avoid assassins, takes the wrong side-street, stops to turn around in front of the disappointed young shooter who had been waiting on the official route and is now headed dejectedly home; the old order already over, a new world exploding into light.

"Karen? You know I love her. Give her this for me and tell her to treat you better."

She quickly – who could have foreseen and yet it was all foreseen, kisses him lightly on the cheek. Time catches its breath, their eyes drink deep. He, as quick, "Give this to Dennis and tell him …" and kisses her on the lips and wait for it, her lips part. She sees a way, right then, right there, to sooth the abrasions caused by Dennis's oscillations. What happens next is the usual man-woman thing, these being frisky, hormone brimming animals in the prime mating years. Sure, it's a betrayal of their partners; that gives it savor. Don't forget the human consolation in it – something almost fine and in certain declensions, decent. At the other polarity of sexuality, the sump pump of lust in action, the waste of spirit in an expanse of shame, a goulash of dimly conceived revenges and frankly pornographic *ecus**. The actual act, a pliable amalgam of compassion and fuck-fest pressed into the cavity of time.

Certainly, when his little man slid past the close portals of her warm, nether lips …

("Oh my god!")

It was Bollinger, PJ and Krug–
It was twist, tango and frug!

It was tiramisu and peaches and cream;
It was every male adolescent's meat beating dream.

It was Pearl Harbor and surrender on the Missouri;
It was "Over the top Marines, Guards and Israeli Golani.'

It was "once more into the breech, once more!"
It was Mother, Virgin, and total whore.
(Strategic advance, total war)

It was mantra, tantra and old Kabbalah;
Touchdown Home team; Raw, Raw Raw!

It was Mauser, Lee-Enfield and Colt,
Screw, washer and bolt.

It was Derrida, Foucault and Deleuze.
It was too tight, too loose and just right.

It was synthetic, analytic and dialectic.
It was slow-fast, vicey versa and frenetic.

New Year's Eve and Fourth of July–
Bright flash, big boom, rockets in the sky!

It was deep night and rising sun;
It was hard work and "Son, job well done."

The deep homing call of whales.
Groaning galaxies, atomic and cosmic scales.

It was sharp blue skies and falling leaves.
It was honor, offer and tease.
(Not in that order).

It was lions, tigers, flying trapezes,
It was radar, ack-ack, diving kamikazes.
Signal pennants snapping in the breeze.

Rap, tap, tickle and slap, rabbit out of hat;
Low blow, clinch, KO and who turned out the light?
And somebody's aria…OK, got it…
Crystal-cracking soprano, "Queen of the Night."

It was life on the run and a cold hard gun;
Picnics and playgrounds and all kinds of fun.

It was *extreme close-up** ("ecu") and the little Guy's perfect "snap"
It was a hard day's shooting and director's "It's a wrap!"

It was Trafalgar, Waterloo and Battle of Britain;
It was offer and honor and new contract written.
(In that order.)

It was Kyrie, Gloria and Credo,
Ha-ha, ah-ah and Oh, Oh! Oh.
Black mass, crazy jazz.

First across the finish line,
Cork pop, gush of wine.

It was "Houston, we have lift-off."
It was clothes tossed first take off.
Footstep, flag stab and claim the moon.

Conjugation! Conjuration! Moments of Moantage.

These couplings could go on and on (theirs did). It was a meaty slice of illicitness, with a dash of danger; nectar from the flower, honey for the hive. Mash it, thrash it. Let copulation thrive.

The Best Lubrication in Bed Is Being Well-read

Young men drinking are talking about women, how so and so is hot and so is another. Naturally one lad proposes having both of them. "A threesome" another exclaims as if a discovery of some new found land, "that's the ultimate". Surveys record that 17% of Americans report a multiple partner sexual experience. Wry commentators add "Proving 17% of Americans are liars." Let us take a less jaundiced view.

In a threesome all are mutually engaged while the structural alternative of two couples is of necessity, distracting and competitive. In the threesome there is an easy axis of alternation and reciprocity. Man in such a situation should achieve a comfortable personal best, one woman being desirable, two being more than arithmetically more so. The arrangement works, theme of a million DVDs.

We see depicted three couples at the banquet, and one man lacking a female partner. She has joined the other lady downstage, assisting a rather conceited and surely contented gentleman out of his excess attire? Are they professionals or is everybody just good friends? Is this an orgy or only a kind of theater, an after dinner entertainment? Do we wish we were there? In what role?

Sex kills time, intensifying duration to the velocity of oblivion. The women, sexually sufficient unto themselves, electing the man's presence as pure phallus, have deeply authenticated him in his being. Being useful that is. What's the old motto – a handyman is worth two of the bush?

As one does, we discussed our former lovers. Why is everyone attracted to these injurious shoals – and yes, she had. Something in my face exposed envy and a kicked puppy's cogitated hurt, so she quickly added "Look, it's not like it was like Plato's Retreat" (note: a famous orgy club, New York of the late 1970s). She paused searching for the right palliative. "It was cuddly." This was too politique for belief, since "cuddly" to the male mind is a sweet syrup incompatible with the hot oils of the erotic. So … it was more "Romper Room" than *Behind the Green Door*? She will always be in that space, the three of them, something about to happen. A dim loser looks on longingly, strategically situated, the observing, the excluded.

A Matter of Taste

Adulterers, for in an adulterated sense that's what Guy and Janet were and rejoiced in believing they were, have all the advantages, timing, and tactics, like those World War Two films. The elite in this case duo of commandos knows all there is to know about the enemy camp, location of the gates and guard house, what hour the sentries change, how they faithfully march always ten yards forward, turn on heel and ten yards back, where the supply, ammo or oil dump is, only the point of this mission is not blow but preserve it even as day by day they raid it, sweating from the risk and reveling in the thrill, fucking on bags of black powder. Not that they care if it blows up (it's a blast!) only they don't want it to blow up, the distinction fine, duplex, definite as is proven by their continuing until it goes blow, as it always does in a palette of Hollywood special effects, bright explosions, burning billows, meteoric shrapnel, careening trucks, belated, desultory shots and shouts, throw in some flares, too late, too late. Anyway, they might have continued through many reels, celebrating their daring (sic) dos with the act itself, accomplished missionary positions varied with 69, woman on top, The Ploughman, Arentino Number 5, rear entry and other inspired improvisations without a known or printable name. Alas, for the fated mistake, a dropped shell casing. So to speak.

Dennis had left work early on Friday, dizzy with the flu. "Don't come by on Saturday" he told Janet "you'll get it." She was offhand, "I'm used to germs." In bed that day he drifted in and out of sleep. He dreamed of life and being well which meant sex with her. At 4 PM she came over, despite his admonition, with ginger ale and a floppy bag of instant chicken soup. His new, post-Karen digs were luxurious compared to the attic if not to the married abode, most of a basement in a leafy neighborhood close to the University, private side entrance with refrigerator and functioning hot pot.

"It's okay, okay" she said as he half waved her away. "We're going to get you better." Seeing her so brisk and solicitous, he felt his desire rise for her and took her arm, pulled her toward the bed.

"No, no" she said, only instead of saying even semi-plausibly "I don't want to catch it" she followed with "I have a yeast infection. Down there."

He laughed it off, replied "I don't care about that. Maybe it will cure me. Maybe a little injection will cure you." For starters he went down on her.

Alone later, even if still feverish, he felt better. His soft illusions revolved around her body, its spicy aromas and agile responsiveness. They had triumphed in each other's arms. He would live. He turned the light out to sleep. His tongue rolled in his mouth, processing an aftertaste of her he couldn't salivate away.

It could only be. Could not be. Must be. Forget it. Yeast she said. Beer, bread in the oven. But he knew that taste, off-almondy with a finish of salty proteinal brine. From boyhood, after the usual solitary experiments, you'd sample the emission with a misson of a million names.

Rocks'offal, jizz, jass, jism, wank. Spanker's Choice; buttermilk, clabber, spilt-milk, fresh squeezed, guy gush, Daddy's gleam. Monk's splet, monkey slime. Penn's oil, seed. Bull's spew, nob glob. Ballburst, shaftblast, love-yum, scum. Penis puke, Sailor's Ale,

Adam's pale, Eve's best drink. Cracks' caulking, wet dream cream, love rush, money spent, ejaculate. Gay-goo, fag-frappe, man juice, male tea, stud mud, white sauce, white spot, bounce-ounce, baby gravy, stain. Breeders'mead, Essence. Hot shot, cum, Moby's muck, in a word sperm, semen, spunk, sprog even if adulterated with the effluent of her love canal and possibly, after all, she had said – a yeast infection. The wise guys in the lit-up offices of his cerebral cortex might be insisting no, no, no, not proven but the no non-sense sanitation men deep in his brain's basement were banging on the pipes Yes, Yes, Yes! Yo bro, somebody been stoking the furnace.

As he settled down to what would be a restless night of non-sleep, the first of many, it flew into his head, an old quote, "mine eyes were not at fault, for she was beautiful, nor my heart that thought her like seeming; it had been vicious to have mistrusted her." Where the fuck did that come from? And an old joke (gag): the police arrive to clean up the mess, not prevent the crime.

A Diversion

Yeah, so here's the suckering brochure. Glossy images, alluring itineraries, "first class posh accommodations on the A deck" type prose.

The serious and the deep author. When the serious sets pen to paper, he tells what he has suffered but the deep one expresses not only what he has suffered but why he lives in current joy.

God, who writes this stuff?

There she goes, the ship, my little crafty vessel, already set sail. Given the known destination I'm not getting on, not even as first tourist. (New title: *First Tourist*). Of course, somebody will argue "It's the journey not the arrival that matters." Which is the whole covenant, contract and conveyance ("writers' rule of three") between authors and readers, isn't it? Listen, been there, done that. Accommodo. [Editor's note. Cf. Henry IV,2, III, ii, 80.]

Because the journey is just another conveyance and the nattering mattering another arrival. Every thought is (an old particular of kant) a vehicle complete in itself and the procession of thoughts, a petty pace through time. [Fine writing]. Who is fooled? Nobody.

No mere sail-billow of rhetoric or Englisyman's irony (Amis and Shandy), I begged you not to go on board. (You must have something better to do and heaven forefend if you don't.) After the easy imaginary posturing, I got down, literally, on my knees and begged you not to. Go back and check. I wept tears seven times salt, attempted to re-launch this lexical liner as SOS *Bark Of Lamentations*. Which would have quashed the whole thing. No one's getting on that weepy-leaky. Cruise cancelled. "We regret we don't to announce …"

But you'll do it your own way and if you've gotten this far, you're outward bound; me, I'm basking onshore, waving a flipper. Bon voyage. I know where you're headed and I don't care.

This is the author's so sought after "voice", pleading, not padding. It's the alchemist negrado, the philosopher's *Der Negative*, the still-null point, the stop at the top of the swing. The Joker in the pack, the black domino. I forget.

[Editor's note. Six weeks after the manuscript was received at WRITES, the author sent an email requesting that a note be added to conclude this section, "Readers should ignore the above section."]

Note: Readers should ignore the above section.

The Little Pine

He'd have to put her under surveillance and stakeout her place. In this he was aided by the slope of nature. For across the curving street from the house where she rented the bottom floor was a vacant lot belonging to someone who didn't want it built on. There it was, periodically mown but with a little wild evergreen about head high, just one of those things, something to do with property, legal reality, conveyances, titles, taxes, who knew. He'd meet her Friday after work, after his radio show (7-10 PM, Dennis was prime time guy on the University's all volunteer classical music station), spend the night and early afternoon with her, declare the rest of the weekend for writing and on Saturday evening jaunt down the road, post himself behind the little pine cedar whatever where he could view the front and side of her house. See whatever he'd see. In the six days that had passed since the Revelation as he called it, it seemed increasing remote that he'd see anything. Everything was so natural between them, forget it. The only change was his intent looking at her when she wouldn't notice. There was no difference in her beautiful pale face except once when she detected his glance.

"Yes?"

"Nothing." Still some small cubic centimeter of his brain retained the taint of taste and would not be denied. He resolved to not shrink from it. Pretend it was war and he was in the army, had to report and do his absurd duty in order to forget about it. That seemed right. Charlottesville in November was mild, warmish. It would get dark soon enough and the hours would pass. Something he'd, they'd laugh about years from now.

Evening fell. He walked down the street to her place something he'd done countless times, never with this studied pretence of non-chalance, deviating a block from her house to take the next cross street and approach his observation post from the rear.

He started standing behind the pine, then awkwardly sat down, shifting for the best view through the branches. Her familiar abode looked strange from this perspective, a place he had never been. His thoughts unspooled, the week's drudgery of taking down the old exhibition, checking and removing items off the on-display list, wrapping packing, insuring and mailing any item loaned, taking the vault boxes out of the vault, fitting the treasures back in, re-shelving them, the first cleaning of the cases and glass in preparation of the new exhibition. How pretty she looked, her long body stretched to remove a book from the back of the flat cases. Next time in bed, wouldn't it be fun to try a new arrangement of rope and knots, to stretch her out. Yes, she liked the occasional recreational restraint. Odd, too the sense elation it gave him to think of her straining against the soft cord. But he couldn't do this job much longer, a year or two max, maybe he'd get the writing fellowship. Maybe he'd get money from Janet's rich uncle because maybe they'd be married. Which was different from marrying her for money, you know. He shifted, his leg was stiff, his butt cramped. Time, nothing much to do with him, ambled. Car headlights played over the lot as they took the curve and Dennis would freeze. He'd read that in war books, don't move in a beam. It was totally ridiculous.

A figure was moving up the street, one he knew before he knew. Guy of the hunched back and limping step, Guy lurching up her stairs who without so much as a look over his shoulder entered as the door opened like magic. Was there a flash of long fingered, elegant hand? The porch light went out, a thing ordinary-extraordinary Dennis couldn't decode. His brain hurt. If the rational lobes had denied the taste while his deep brain was certain, now surged a voltic reverse, the white collar cells in the corner office coolly concluding Guy was the guy while the maintenance men in the basement refused to believe it, sending up to the front office limbic surges of disbelief that were dutifully translated into reasonable refutations. Surely he'd see his two friends leave in a few minutes to go to his place – and he wouldn't be there! He half-laughed, that would be his little revenge for their putting him though this. His minor merriment halted at the image of them pressed flesh to flesh, a thought he had never had. Minutes became spatial, that is they just got deeper. How many, how deep? What were they doing in there? Extraordinarily, all the lights died. The house blinked like a cat, looked at him unperturbedly with its night eyes. Temporality ceased. He was falling, falling. There was no bottom.

As he fell, his mind went red with resolution. He'd kick the door down, throw Guy down the stairs, bruise and brand her with bitter words of what she was. But could he control his rage? Things would get out of hand. At that mental word, he looked down at his hands to see a faint blue light flicking over them like wisps of cooking gas. It was totally weird and completely natural. It was the power to kill, a savage electricity potentialized in his arm, imminent, gathering to be discharged. A very clear voice popped into his head. "No one must die." A last hope, "Must be the fuses", flared and sputtered.

He grasped the little pine's branches. The needles stung his hands, pressing tighter, his vision went blurry from tears. He thought "I will kill this tree, leave it cursed, twisted, stunted, poisoned to the roots. Bitch, bitch, bitch." Suddenly he was very tired, his being beaten. He stumbled home in a stupor that might have lasted hours or just one long moment, dry heaved over an obliterated reflection in the toilet. Went to bed, fidgeting with thoughts of direst cruelty. Punched the tear-damp pillow. No sleep, no sleep. Around dawn in semi-delirium, he thought a vicious wood pecker with claws dug in his shoulder, pecked at his ear. He tried to knock it off. It shrieked "She's easy, she's easy." He knew that bird; the hard faced girl at the party.

The little tree hadn't noticed him. It had no receptivity for human passion. Its vital awareness was for sun, water, a little square of earth where it grew and flourished until ten years later the frat boys chopped it for their tertiary Christmas bole and two weeks after threw it still bravely green onto the street, needles showering at the heft.

Ties that bind

Dennis was perfectly blind sighted, blindsided. Sex was good with her (and for her). So everything was alright, right? Sure he took Janet for granted. So what? People do. We mustn't make the shame mistake,

She wasn't settled in her sexuality and this obviated her capacity for loyalty. At her elite women' s college, she'd cut quite a figure, the epicene Dona Juana of her class, a one woman missionary for Sappho, making her an embarrassment to the administration and every hetero-normative parent's nightmare ("I told you we should have gone co-ed!)

After graduation, a year study of archeology (not classics) at Columbia where she expeditiously delved into men; a jacket off the shoulder, concept glib Euro-pseude met at a reception at the Met, a fellow student excavator in the bosky margins of an Anglo-Saxon bog. She could take them or leave them (as she could New York).

Dennis, surprisingly, was to her taste. Conversantly "well" read, polite with a sheathed edge, maybe. She had tested him, chats at work. She could see it – go to bed with the husband, go to bed with the wife whom she knew from classes and frankly favored. Which is exactly what happened, like one of the books she relished, contorted plot, tangled bodies and emotions, middle Murdoch. The total bonus, she liked Dennis in bed. He was urgent, demanding, harsh. Physically, he filed her up. She was amused by the alteration: Dennis, anxious, over mannered librarian in the stacks, was a barbarian in the sack. (As later she would be by Guy, imperious Bonaparte of the bistros, cuddy cupid cooing in bed). These men, these men! [Editor's note. Cf. *Othello*, Act IV, iii, 60-61]

Dennis got the idea of ropes, where? Brain aromas rising from a testosteronic stew of porn, D'Sade, Swinburne and some X-rated book plates yellowing in the Special Collections erotica files, nothing more natural, books and binding. Anyway, a trip to the hardware store (and boy was he looking forward to her hardware) for soft synthetic cord gave ample frame for mental debate – should he ask her permission? Nah, that was daft. A behavioral oxymoron. He cut the stuff into manageable fourths, practiced a few knots secured to the bed legs, stuffed the segments under the pillows and next time she came over, stretched her out, rigged her up. Surprised, she held a sharp intake of breath, was game, gamy. It worked for her, shivered her timbers.

Climbing the rise of her climax, she was always pushing against an enabling resistance that featured the sudden pivot and reverse of force in her favor. Pulling against the ropes augmented her push back, increased the amplitude of erotic swing. She leapt off the plank into deep release. She forgot all about Dennis (who pranced around afterwards like a master of ceremonies.) She forgot herself.

It was too good to diminish by overuse. Once every third Saturday of the third month was the trick.

One other thing was connected with the ropes, a thing unspeakable not because it was sordid but because it was sacred. Sorta sacred.

It was a week later (the rota not yet established), right after their second session, Saturday 5 PM. Attuned to a worker's schedule, they were hungry and brisk with success. Splash bathing in the sink, they quickly dressed and headed out to their favorite restaurant,

"Random Row", a half hour walk along University Avenue transitioning into Main Street.

Ten minutes down the road, they were stopped at a corner waiting for a light. It changed, they stepped out, Janet glanced at the cars starting up on her right. Attached to some metaphysical elastic, as they accelerated, they slowed. There was no category for her comprehending her perception. The cars were static in motion, like bubbles in an oversized level, moving and confined. Zeno's arrow, *Alice Through the Looking Glass*, the Red Queen going faster and faster, going nowhere was as close as she could get to it. Even as they passed her, she was always ahead of them as if looking down from a temporal height. Still walking, she looked to the next light's sequencing. From the red going off to the green going on took an eternity, a growing gap in nature. Now she could detect even as all objects appeared normal, a frolic of atoms choreographing the grain of solidity, a back ground radiation to visual form pricking her retina, nothing she could literary see. She turned to Dennis who was staring at her.

"Time…" He finished it for her, "has stopped."

When they got to the restaurant, there'd been touches to temporal frame, a myriad of small adjustments back to true. They passed through the entrance's air lock into warmth and voices, were seated, studied the familiar menu, a manual to the real world they had reentered:

Spanokopteia. A traditional Greek pie with a tasty spinach and feta cheese filling, served with brown rice or risotto and your choice of additional side or salad. A vegetarian favorite.

Random Burger. Six ounces of USDA certified angus beef on our famous fresh made bun and your choice of cheeses, bacon lettuce and tomato, cooked the way you like it OR or let us Randomly surprise you.

Spaghetti milanesi. Our own daily made pasta, blended with a tangy tamarind tomato sauce, topped by a generous and savory four cheese garnish, all baked to perfection. Choice of side or salad.

She waited for him to speak.

"It happened to you?"

"Yes"

"Time stopped", he repeated. Nothing framed it, nothing touched it, nothing else to say.

When it was no longer too delicate for words, they easily concluded that some neurochemical had crested up or drained out from the sex and that twenty-five minutes later it had re- or discharged. Which didn't really explain it, the identical simultaneity. She, who had read more widely than her professors, couldn't think of a like incident in literature. He agreed. Pilar's "the Earth moving" was nothing compared to time's quarter of an hour stoppage.*

A year later, Guy asked what she and Dennis did in bed. He wanted to know and didn't need to insist, no shyness modifying her reply. Perhaps he'd come up with something new. No, he wanted to do what they'd done.

"Let me tie you up."

Serenely, with soft voiced definitude, she said no (And said it the six more times he asked but it was only the first time mattered.) She was capable of loyalty after all.

In Heaven there was exultation and joyful noisings, Non nobis and Te deum. Choirs of angles clapped their wings as the brightest amongst them, bracelets bright upon the up borne arm, tapped a golden tambourine. Because God loves the black sheep and the black swan and at the utterance of her "no" she was both.

---

*Months later she would reflect how there had been nothing paradisiacal about the experience except its essence — the suspension of time. For the Fall of Man is the falling into time and time's cessation, redemption. Time, she decided, symbolically stops in tragedy's extremist cathartic realizations, real events, an idea she would use in her dissertation.

Now you'd be thinking, you haven't given Guy his say. And we're not going to. But in all fairness, we are going to give him his due. Here goes …

Thirteen Ways of Looking at a Guy

> "Guy was walking in the autumn winds. He too was a part of the pantomime."
>
> — *Wallace Stevens.*

His Art

In this period, one could observe all three phases of his artistic production. First, from college, a number of mid-sized and garish acrylic canvases where distressed humanoid plankton were suspended in an odd, unresolved multi-perspectival space that was vaguely Chinese-Roman. Then his "middle-period" oils, as prior described, weird skyscrapers built upon "water lilies", Bosch clobbers Monet somewhere west of Piranesi.

Lastly, on long 8 x 3 foot panels of thin translucent paper, squares, cubes, torqued rectangles floating swirling dancing ("A musical notation that is music."— Guy Mantis) drawn with black marker, a pattern of patterns flowing forward like a river, at no point beginning or ending.

Later he recognized they had, for all his ingenuity, something of the quality of a simple transcript, the tones of her, rising, falling, building again, cresting, the curl of wave braking into laughing foam.

This was not the only recording or registration of her undulating action. The law student who shared an apartment bedroom wall with Guy quickly picked up on their tune ups, learned their timings and would jack-off to her deep throated tones, an instrumentalist following a score, like any old time Morse coder fisting out his transmission of strokes and splashes, dashes and dots, __ __ __ __ __ __ __ __ __ __ .__ o o o o

Sometime the three or four of them would pass on the exterior stairs and Dennis, ever alert to protect his woman, definitely didn't appreciate the way Law II leered at Janet.

Dennis to Guy: "You tell him, politely, that if he looks at her like that again, I'm going to knock his block off."

Guy to Dennis: "No prob, I'll handle it."

His Proposal

Sitting in his cavernous brown naugahyde recliner, (inherited from his father, still retaining a faint sweet whiff of the old man), Guy was slump shouldered and looking Lincolnish, mediating on the deep antinomies of history (*his* history; another fuck, another painting lost.). The third of his thoroughly read (including "Sports" and "Business" sections which he had no interest in) carefully folded Washington Post columns (as in architecture) was half way to the ceiling. "When it gets there, I think I'll make my little proposal to Janet." Four months later, balanced on the third step of a rattling but entirely sound aluminum step ladder, as he slid the daily detritus in (Jan 22 1983) between the top paper (yesterday's Jan 21) and the egg white stippled stucco, touching the ceiling, he recalled his intention and decided not to.

Eight months after, another cyclical tick off. The calendar's curl of their first night, prima nocta when the moon was high, the harvest swelling and human hormones at the surge. He was at first bemused then perplexed at the conventionality – he of all people, a man obliged (Desi Arnez, Eddie Albert, Wilbur Post, Dick van Dyke more like) to recognize an "anniversary". She, the cause of this existential embarrassment, deserved a little of it tossed back at her. When she arrived as arranged, he said "You know, we really ought to tell Dennis – and Karen too. Then we ought to get (he was careful not to say "let's") married. Tell them after." She paused, her trim thoughts doing a brisk galliard, the refrigerator humming its reliable base line. Her reply –

"No. We can't destroy what we have, what we've made, this, she gestured, her urgent lovely hand conjuring space. I'm afraid of the change. Think of the consequences. Aren't you happy?" (This is known as Updike's Negative.)

"Oh God, yes. I'm so tired of this, the deception. It's not right. It's suffocating us. I feel cheap. Yes, yes, yes ..." falling into his spindly arms. (This is known as Updike's Positive.)

What she really said was:

"You must be kidding."

"I was."

His Song

There the three or four of them would be in his car, Guy driving and suddenly he'd break into song, rousing up a fair faux Robesonian baritone "Bess, you is my woman now." Two of them didn't get it at all, he was just being goofy, his irrepressible if unpredictable high spirits. Janet got it and would chide him when they were alone.

"I want you to stop singing. Stop singing *that*."

"Why? I like to sing."

"I won't have you making fun of him that way."

"Bird gotta fly, man gotta sing."

"The next time you do, I won't let you have me." She was stern only so far, like a school teacher with a recalcitrant child.

So he pledged not to do it again and did the next time he felt like it, driving them all back from the Chinese restaurant, stopped at a light. Later, she didn't deny him because, quite simply, she didn't want to.

(How simple it would have been, the quick flick of a switch since the signal that the coast was clear with no Dennis docked was her porch light on, a beam Guy homed in on.)

His Endearments

He come over as arranged, at 7 PM exactly and at 7:05 PM was pacing back and forth because she was sitting on the bed's edge in her light gown that accented her lovely shoulders, calmly doing the TLS crossword. The radio was on low, the chamber music show, 7-9 PM, tuned to 91.3 FM, the university station.

"Can't you do that later?"

"I'm just about to finish (*Cunning Venetian, five letters, ending with "e"*) which I will do a lot faster if you sit still and clam up."

He threw himself in her chair and began picking his thumbs. 7:08 the first piece of music ended, some tid-bit, Mendelssohn's *On Wings of Song*. Dennis's voice emanated from the box in full FM vox, giving the performance credits and intro to the next piece. It was all beautifully convenient.

Minutes passed. Guy gloomed. Janet with her pencil attacked the paper. If they had been listening, they weren't, they'd have heard the first theme's beginning development.

Guy cleared his throat, ready for a little development of his own.

"How's it going, Trixie?"

"Trixie?"

"Trixie is my pet name for you." He let it sink in. "Because you're so tricky."

She was angry. "Tricky. Because I turn tricks. Listen buster, despite being a little weak in the loyalty line, I'm nobody's whore."

"You coulda fooled me." He grinned.

"You bastard." She threw the magazine at him, her face white with rage.

He met her gaze directly, then bounding from the chair, was on his knees, his head in her lap.

"Forgive me, forgive your little Guy. I'm sorry, I'm sorry, our time together is so precious, I can't stand to see it pass like this. Forgive, forgive." He hugged her leg, looked up to her closed eyes with their cruel Baltic line.

"Alright, but don't ever call me that again."

Even as she lightly stroked his hair, she was determined to make him work harder and he, of necessity, would work her harder. It was usually this way after their spats. He mused if she knew he engineered them, if she was complicit in a process that sharpened their pleasure, as the music reached its finale and Dennis's plumy voice made the announcements: the piece, the performers and, as a public service, a litany list of lost dogs and cats. (One night, I swear – truth is too perfect for fiction, there was a lost cat, "Trixie" but Guy and Janet *really* weren't listening.)

His Generosity

Guy, you may have gathered from the stacked newspapers and dancing musical cubes, was naturally neat; he understood, especially after Karen had taken him in her care, that a creep in bad clothes (paint splattered white shirt and jeans) is a just a creep while a creep in good trim is an item of interest so you need to see him in his bone-fided Bean brand brown loafers, with their recess on the tongue for a bright penny, the Perma Press chinos and Oxford clothe shirts, the suede jacket for the light cold, the camel hair for deeper and a factory reject Burberry discounted sans label, fully equipped with capes and pockets for war and all seasons in between, which was over the top if making quite a statement, all topped off by a natty black Greek fisherman's hat from the rear of which our friend's lank fair hair furled girlishly and beguilingly. (Did I mention the touch of not a touch too much Old Spice?) I say "our friend" because you are beginning to like him and no shame in that; it's just natural, describe someone, present them in situations and that old human warmth will bubble up reliable like Mr Geyser; golly, shucks, he aint so bad. Got some good qualities actually. Take Hitler: a Boy Scout in lederhosen decorated War Vet, an up and comer who takes care about his appearance, loves animals, *is* vegan, has fascinating eyes, can discourse knowledgeably about all kinds of good music and historical stuff. Loyal to the friends he's loyal to, too. *He's not all bad–* just in the wrong place. Like Guy. And brave (I mean Guy but yeah, Hitler too). Brave in a pure ferric blood line going back to Saxo or Hanno whomever, some snotty nosed serf in rags with guts and gumption enough to say we're getting the hell out of Baron Otto's shit sty, going over the river boys where we don't see anybody and gets our own land. So they did, crossing a lot of rivers, always bumping into somebody until they got to Transylvania, a pretty little dale there and standing down the local Slavs also already there (only there'd been a plague so not so many of them) because in those crummy medieval battles once you ran you were meat (chopped and pulped) and they didn't and so made it their happy valley for 500 years until 1944 when the Red Army rolled in, rollicking and raping.(Which event his father missed, being a bone-fide American, *his* father (Guy's grand) having the good idea of getting out of the mittel-europe cauldron, achieved, via Ellis Island in 1910, where the fine old by then Transylvanian-saxon Heldenvolk name of "Manstch" became on official papers and ever after "Mantis" which didn't bug anyone, being easily spelled and rather more American or at least Tex-Mex sounding.) And was generous (our Guy) let me tell you how.

Very neatly arranged under his bed, just fitting, were ten archival boxes, measuring 12 x 17 x 8, made of ANSI certified low acid cardboard, with neat metallically hinged covers, the same kind used at the library to hold the foul papers (which is a technical term) of Faulkner and Hem and Dos and, in the latter days, Orr and Davenport, Casey and Beattie and other tenured epigones, tons of scribbles, letters, recipes, notes for novels, notes for notes of novels (oh yes), actual novels, first, last and every draft in between, landscaping bills and IRS worksheets (pre-TurboTax, natch), the cumulative tax write-off for this pulp greater than anybody was paid for anything published, (not to mention value as raw recycling), in just such neat receptacles was arranged in chronological order within titles, Guy's collection of *Playboy, Hustler, Honcho, Prime Cut, Galore* and *Gash*, not to mention, rare items from DC's finest purveyors of pornography just west (typo "wets") of the capitol, from the black curtained back room, higher priced private stock of *Euro Sluts, Licking Lesbos* ("Best Of") and *Dungeon Master XXX*. Guy'd take a worn out issue, ("lovingly thumbed" as they say in the book trade) roll it up, secure it with rubber bands bow and stern, insert a plastic bag liberally coated with not for much longer pure virgin olive oil and pressing it into the iron ribs which is to say thighs of his bedroom radiator, insert his personal piston in the slick cylindrum (the LubeTube, a wonderfully satisfying device, patent pending with satisfaction guaranteed not that we can return your wad if you haven't spent it or especially if you have) not as good as being a bee (one of them) in "Trixie's" honey comb for which he need keep a sting, an edge because she was one protestant hard ass – you might be one of her Elect but she made you work hard for your spurt of salvation and the exultation of her revelations, this whore of bib-bib-Babylon.

Once a month he'd go over to Dennis's basement room bearing gifts, five or six tried tested (if not yet Lube-tubed) issues from his now decidedly curated collection. The idea being that Dennis working *his* edge off would result in said donor getting an opening for a bonus night with "Trixie", now averaging 1.8 sessions a week. In a sense, he was simply being generous; if he was costing Dennis a groaning, this was some compensation. "Here take these, I'm wearing my pecker out" which was true enough if not in the way Dennis supposed, Guy's being one of those little pencils they give out at libraries or put-put golf courses, one he kept sharpened having asked her, in a moment of post-triste-ish candor if she, the bone fide Venus Velvet of smoothest graphite, liked the way his little attorney filed motions in her high court of appeal, she replying loftily like a supreme hussy-justice (in her gauzy black nightglow down right magisterial, barely disarranged) doing the interpretive queen of corona on some masticable quidibble of law, "It's not the size that matters, it's the steadfastness" which was, he thought, a beautiful way to put it, noble even, like Portia's great speech of which he was reminded ("the quality of pussy is not strained, it moistens as the gentle rain, it is twice blessed, it blesseth him that takes and she that gives, it is tightly with the mightiest …") which riff we might totally agree with you (imagined reader) is an over the top, under the garter belt bit of disagreeable show boating that violates every formal fictional decorum; of voice, of register, not to mention good taste, yep, all wrong except – hold that notion, Norton, *we aren't depicting, we are demonstrating.* This isn't a picture, it's a manufactured object that transmits the proscribed vibes: the discomfort you feel is what Guy *was--*, freakish and frankly unpleasant (by luck and locale my friend, whom I'm faithful to in a way he'd appreciate) because this isn't fiction, it's history-remember, you read that a longtime ago on page six and if you didn't what are you doing here anyway and if you did and forgot, I can only say it's better readers we require, not writers. In history, any testament, testimony, deposition, view, memoir and interview of participants long after the fact is admissible, however heterogeneous, in order to give best apprehension of events distant not for purposes antiquarian (my granddaddy's daddy took San Juan Hill so where did he put it ha-ha-ha we don't care) or predictive or instructive (learn from history? Look at the body count, we have, we have, *too successfully*) –- but for the pure impure human too human beauty of it, a bloodied well wrought urn, the golden bowl cracked and if only for being too comprehensively by which we mean comprehendedly pressed in hand, broken.

His best quality was courage and it takes courage too to praise your worst enemy as in this rarefied treatment *Thirteen Ways of Looking at a Guy*, go ahead and count 'em, thirteen, *guaranteed.*

Though candidly, this is the most boring, for you, for me, writing I've ever done and if you say "Whoa, you can't say that" may I remind you that such observations are inadmissible only in fiction (reliant on a weak scaffold of plausible invention), not in history with its high tensile strength quiddity, which I repeat this is. If you are offended by being so chastised and addressed, may I suggest you write your own history or fiction or whatever, that includes in its narrative the efficient cause (Aristotle, Aquinas et al.) of its own creation, namely that I again annoyed you by again addressing the issue of history versus fiction which, you should concede, is game, set and match, in the name of the Father, Son and Holy Ghost. Amen.

His Fear

Alone, after finishing a painting, he'd hear the blood thrusting in his ears (early carotid clog?) smell the burnout under his arms. Death was getting closer every moment, and not in the common sweep of time, no, in the way a second hand stops on one thin indicator, for a mortal eon, for a second, before moving onto the next, the utterly other. Youth fears death with nauseating intensity.

Even if his involvement with Janet was discovered and Dennis freaked out and tried to kill him it was better than just sitting in that room, his visual field full of inert objects, done art, bereft, ready to be left. Karen, Janet, even a 200 lb. diabetic parolee from Star Hill, would serve his distracting turn.

Naturally, he took reasonable precautions, always carrying a small seven shot Beretta. He had also made a point of waving around the latest *Post* story about a "romantic triangle murder" in DC, interrogating Dennis on the general theme. Guy: "Serves them right. Cheating on a guy like that, right?" Dennis: "Nope, I don't agree. It's not right to kill for that." Guy: "Why not?" Dennis: "Because it's a, what — infraction *within* life, it's not like self-defense or defending your culture. Kill for adultery? We'd be stepping over bodies to work." Guy sighed, "If I'm ever in that situation, I hope you are the husband." Which even Dennis thought was a peculiar thing to say and which really was a hilarious, worthy-of-Restoration theatre trope-a-dope of double dealing, n'est-ce pas?

His Manners

In any human transaction, "please and thank you" were not part of his vocabulary. For instance, he enjoyed eating out and being served. If his order arrived when he was in full conversational spate, he'd discourse and wouldn't hesitate to flag down the server later to demand that his food be warmed. When one came round to enquire "how are you all doing?" (eating is a job?) he'd speak first and command "more coffee" or "another sloe screw ...driver"(which he just happened to like and was super conveniently, during his involvement with Janet, a coded request). Never a "thank you" when the check came so that finally Dennis, or Karen or Janet, all of them or one of them, felt obliged to criticize him. Meaning the next time they ate out, when the check came, he pronounced loudly and sententiously, emphasizing each syllable, THANK YOU. Guy's companions rolled their eyes at the waiter who got it – "just another nutter." He never tipped; that was left for his friends to do who over did in compensation.

Why did Karen, Janet, Denis put up with him? Because they were young and friendship in youth is exploratory, based on large allowances, tolerances and frankly, curiosity.

Nor is it not *quite* true to say he never tipped. If the waitress was handsome and kept her composure, he'd pull out of his wallet his "Virginia National Bank Vest-pocket Tip Calculator Card" that listed every amount from five to fifty dollars in fifty cent increments next to columns of 4-10-15-20%. Guy was a determined four per center. Except once when they all watched as he placed four one dollar bills on the cleared table and with fast fingers deftly folded them into a long winged bird, a tiger or puma or cat, a bull and a sitting midget in a bishop's miter. Later, it was Dennis, his night with Janet, who asked "What was that all about?" as a preliminary to his own answer, "Portraits. Totems of us. He be the man, of course, of course, Karen the flighty bird, you the cat, which makes me, ah, the bull." Dennis made finger horns on his head. "Torro, torro, torro." Janet for once couldn't resist a double take, nodded. They agreed that whatever it was about, it had been charming, almost magical, that little stand of animals. And if that was what it took for him to contribute so handsome a gratuity (on a $25 check), bravo.

His Vital Data

Full Name: Guy Maximilian Mantis

DOB: Nov. 22, 1951

Place of Birth: Arlington, Va.

Ht.: 5,4"

Wt. 125lbs

Hair: Blonde

Eyes: Seaweed Green

Blood Type: O

Cock (Erect): Four and a half inches

Education, BA, MA (English, University of Virginia.)

Favorite author: none

Favorite book: *Notes from the Underground* by Dostoevsky.

Favorite composer: Mozart

Favorite piece of music: Mozart's Piano Concert No. 21 in D minor

Favorite artist: da Vinci

Occupation: Part- time graduate student, and clerical worker; artist.

Hobbies: Chess, old TV sitcoms, pornography and put-put golf.

Alcohol: yes

Meat: yes

Drugs: no

Women: yes

His Drives

He worked 4 to 8 PM (M,W,F) as the library's check desk clerk, sitting at a card table at the entry-exit, examining each patron's books to see that it had an approved stamped due date from the circulation desk because the library's "tattle-tape" spine embedded security strip, desensitized at checkout, wasn't perfect. There been an expensive study (worth about fifty years of security strips or five thousand books) conducted by a conflicted of interest consulting agency proving that without a check person the library could lose hundreds of books year which was reason to invest another two million in improved security strips from an affiliated company. Not a bad job, he could read and when he got off, he'd often go for a long drive, a thing he'd always enjoyed and now more than ever as increasingly his non-work evenings were, shall we say, "booked".

He had no regular route. One night, it might be Monticello Road passing the hicks' shopping center at "Pantops" with its illuminated makes-your-skin crawl-large low plastic dome, a vaguely Jeffersonian oversized vaginal cap, marking the limit of regular city traffic. A nice stretch of free highway led to the intersection with interstate 64, and twenty-five minutes South later, another intersection with Route 250 which he could take home. The constant low level concentration for driving was relaxing, it occupying some place where otherwise sprouted his tangled concerns and boy, let's be fair, did he have them, concerning Karen and Janet and Dennis and all the usual under thirty-two year old stuff about money, meaning and the future. After about fifteen minutes in the car, his mind cleared for what he called "Great Thoughts". Once or twice Janet had accompanied him sitting in the back, quite the properly chauffeured madam while he solilo-quized only it just wasn't as good. He preferred talking to himself and he needed isolation to accelerate, 55-65-75 and speeds above which his old 1973 Cutlass Supreme engine fired imperfectly as a tang of gas snaked up through the vents and pedal ports, a smell he liked.

Tonight it mingled with residue of Janet's spicy oil, slowly evaporating from lap heat, off his thoroughly dipped stick. (He got a fifteen minute break at the job, which earlier he had extended to a job risking forty five, conveying thusly to Janet his urgency and need, which she had graciously recognized and quickly gratified). He felt good. He could conceive (the little roadside cedars of the going back-to-woods abandoned small holdings sequencing in his side vision like a primitive Winsor McCay cartoon) of dying except he could *only* conceive it. His body told him it was impossible he would die. He was motoring in Great Thought Territory now. The universe was strange. Physically organized, likely a fluke. Think of all the non universes, the still born, cosmic abortions. Physics was not indicative of any deeper meaning (as Einstein knew, is at most foundational, the quantum, it was indicative of chaos). Humans made meaning with their games, procedures, rules and laws; boy scout versions of the only thing that mattered, Art. And artists? Taxonomically, they were madmen with method, over brimming with ideas, conceits, plans, out of control crazy stuff. In control Schizos. Then there were lovers, likewise fantastical, fashioning a more circumscribed cosmos or object, the beloved; Dennis's blank face of trust flashed into his mind. And what was he himself, taking a glance in the rear-view mirror, but a lover endowed with all the fabled powers of perception and endurance, better than his clueless friend. He hadn't been ill, no cold, flu, not even a tooth cavity, for over a year. He needed less sleep, was never tired. He was a god. Which is to say less than an artist (which he also was) who endowed with the madman's fecundity and the idolizer's focus, is the greatest being in the universe. Especially if he is *actually* a lover *and* a bit of a madman. Teasing 80 MPH now, the engine pounding, the chassis shuddering, he was way outrunning his headlights (an illuminating cone flattened out into a bright screen, ten feet in front of his bumper) and really, in a just universe of a caring God, should have been arrested as a matter of public safety even on that empty road except that the on-patrol officer, Sheriff Seth Shifflet, cannily parked in the feeder lane where it was covered by culvert, who in twenty years of duty had ticketed so many hundreds of students, good ole boys and joy riding colors that folks joked the new county office building annex should be called the Shifflet Wing, was having radio reception trouble with the small FM outlet (Crozet and only seventy watts) that was broadcasting the big game, Lane High Presidents versus traditional red neck rivals the Nelson Rebels on the night Seth Jr. (called "Junior" at home) was starting at quarter back for the Rebs because Jim Morris had broken his ankle the week before, and Seth senior, everything you'd want in a father in the two hundred pound law enforcement line, wasn't going to miss that game when deputy Purvis would happily have taken the shift except his wife was having a baby and so he didn't see Guy hurtling pass or care to hear (why he had posted himself on this low-traffic stretch to begin with) the over 65 mph "please take notice" beep from his side mounted Ajax (next-to-last-model made in the USA) radar gun so that Guy was able not only to finish his thought but articulate it, gazing grimly on the road with fisherman's cap brim firmly fixed just above his brows to frame a Flying Dutchman focus. "The madman, the lover and the Artist ... I am he", concluding this session of Great Thoughts with a laugh theatrical, semi-maniacal: hee-hee-hee.

His Sublimations

The reason Guy looked none too handsome, honest, was that both his parents looked only average and he the downside combo, that and the fact that his mother had had a few drinks, nothing excessive, just enough to sooth her frustration with her ever fastidious husband (one of *those,* by which I don't mean gay I mean anal) the night right after he was conceived, the Beefeater hitting the innocent zygote hard. The fetching limp was due to an over brisk forceps pull by the obstetrics resident at Arlington General. The baby presenting in the breech position, what else could he do?

If you looked odd people treated you odd and you become odder which is one kind of fated destiny, I'd say. He was badly bullied, not so much in elementary school where old style school marms who recognized the problem could mother hen him, as during the two years of junior high. In those days, Arlington still had rough areas, low income shack zones near the Oxymoron Industrial Park and nothing gave the Camel packing, Brill cream slicking, vocational course lads more pleasure than preying on the weak. It was bad, arm twisting shakedowns for lunch money, pushing school books off the hip, glasses snatching and random punches where they wouldn't show. The ringleader was Moses Mahone, who truth to tell even at fourteen had a kind of young Brando gangsterish charisma (which didn't save him from being drafted a few years later and having a leg blown off by a VC redeployed Claymore near Fukat) found delight in having his victims, Guy his special favorite, address him as "uncle" as in "Thank you, uncle" after a limb numbing punch to the upper arm or "Sure uncle, if you'd like to inspect my terrarium that I've worked on for weeks to get the vital balance right for my biology project and smash it on the ground, which I will certainly explain was my fault entirely for tripping, that's fine with me, uncle."

The anticipation of each day was horrible; he could hardly get out of bed. What to do? It came to him to him one night watching an episode of the Beverly Hillbillies, featuring Mae West as guest star who was vamping everybody she met, including the gentle Jethro. Lesson and use: People would do anything for sex and Guy could draw anything. In terms of technique, bodies, from panting peaks at medical texts in the public library, not to mention keyhole ambuscades of his bathing mother, bodies he could manage, erotic postures and expressions he was way less sure of. The women had to *look* right and he didn't have time to figure it out. Solution: he hurried on down to Sabato's Pharmacy to buy an issue of *Argosy* (or was that *Stag*?). Now no law bidding decent store would sell a young lad *Playboy* (the girls looked too nice & normal) but no problem about a "men's adventure" mag, like *Stag* (or *Epic*), sure to put hair on the lad's chest (haw haw haw) and juice him up for Nam, Korea, West Berlin and other gimlet eyed watch-walls of Freedom, with their no nonsense reporting of real events … "I was a prisoner of the All Gal SS" or "Susi Wong, Queen the of the South Sea Pirates", each red-blooded issue richly (60%) illustrated with nubile women in considerable legally decent disarray, i.e. tattered skirts, blouses off the shoulder, all about three minutes from various fates worse than death or alternatively (40%), constrained All-American guys, William Holden types about to get a graduate degree in Marquis de Sade quality exquisite hurt via their own bodies and or their inability to defend their gal pals'. Here is the time for a significant reflection on how great artists create expressions: how Botticelli's Venus (from *Mars and Venus*) with her gentle triumphant glance of comeuppance had never before been seen in woman's face, though after, ordinary daughters of fallen Eve worked hard to emulate it and so it entered into the suite of actual countenance. If Guy as a young lad couldn't out do a Botticelli, some instinct instructed him that Moses, like most bullies, wanted to be bullied (just as – a scandalous statistic nobody wants to talk about, a sizable percentage of the bullied become compensatory brutes themselves, mid-management tyrants, captains of industry or just another other side of cube shit) and so the first drawing he completed and presented to Moses (the offer, natch, being "more where this came from if you leave me alone and give protection from others") depicted a tied to the stake nude dude (slightly resembletive, with oyster shell ears and broad brooding shoulders, of Moses himself) being flogged by bush skirted pigmies while their semi-safari garbed ivory queen, luminous from self basting lubrication, sat spread leg on a bamboo throne with the proud mien, firm lipped and arched brow (and bouffant, Clarol box photo hair) come hither look of one who has been around and come out on top. This was Guy's first payment in protective call it portraiture and he had no problem producing thirty (pencil and charcoal) more that kept Moses so happy that the Attila of the middle school margins began to lose bully buff and "heavy" cred. One sure would like to see the whole portfolio since that first drawing (imagine all the others!) was a perceptive precursor (if not Botticellish producer) of the *very* look, cunning and imperious, that Janet took on whenever she decided to indulge her femme fatality, itself the product of … everything is connected, innit?

His Animadversions

He was an able, gentle lover, which surprised both "his" women because they had no expectation of any kind except a possible threshold of weirdness. He was like an erotized baby, petting, caressing and unlike a baby in his calibrated technique, responsiveness and generosity.

Being in bed with a warmed up, naked woman was to him an inching towards blissful union with an all accepting, all approving sexualized mother, his anger and resentments appeased and obliterated in the act. After climax, always simultaneous, he'd roll off into the nook of arm, close his eyes and give little coos in his breath's hollow, a desiring child (his tonsorial fringes and small frame confirmatory details) who'd shed with the drop and kick of clothes adult armor; the cynical and assertive opinionator, the Bonaparte of the bistros, always "right" and always "in your face", transformed, gentled by sex, fulfilling too a subverted instinct in these childless women. This was the magic cove, twenty-five minutes of human time. Soft seas, island breezes. The scents of Clorets (him) and sated secretions.

Then a sudden shift of resting bodies, and with an asserting remark '("Lets do it again." Or "I bet the neighbors heard that." or "What time is it?" when the clock watched a glance away on the table) he was Richard the Third after an unthwarth hiatus, suddenly "himself again."

Janet was for him sexual supplement, toy, danger, victory. Karen was the real thing. He responded deeply to her softness, blondeness and sweet under odor (Janet was astringent and briny). They were the same size. She was incremental, less explosive in the act and he preferred that. (Frankly, he despised Janet's able-bodied duplicity who bore, in that regard, the onus for both of them. She was his partner in conspiracy and what did that tell you? For another thing, she was keeping her options open. Despite the compliment of her alliance in betrayal, Dennis, dutiful and dumb, was still the main chance.) While for Karen, in their good period (a year?), he was the only option.

She appreciated and responded to his art. They enjoyed games; mahjong, Go and especially chess where her advantage in natural intelligence was countered by his knowledge of standard openings and end-games. So many pleasant hours around the boards, moves punctuated by chat, the light, teasing touch of hands. (Look, Dennis after losing a game to her in a four move "fools mate" had thrown the wooden board to the floor and crushed it. Nice guy.) Here, in their everyday relations, Guy's arrogance was an asset. Smart she was (a flattery to him), with creative efforts limited to decorations of colored string, patterns turned upon tacks on board or the intricate tartan patterns she invented on her loom. He didn't care, these things didn't challenge him. As noted, the sex worked. Why, this might have gone on forever or at least to setting up house and marriage because many a marriage has been made on less than shared pleasure in a good forty move game of chess.

Except she couldn't ignore, as Dennis could, his arrogance. He was too frequently telling her what to read, what music to listen to, good uses of her time. One evening she put Mahler Five on the stereo; it symbolized to her catastrophe and resurrection, her own. Quiet he was for a quarter hour after. She thought he was moved. The spell broke, he was angry, dissecting Mahler's musical metastases, illuminating the violations of sonata structure and crass orchestration. Resolved not to debate him, she rose when he cited "Jewish indulgence."*

"Jewish?"

He waved his hand dismissibly. "Musical not racial. Didn't you hear the Klezmer, Ashkenazi jazz? You know what Adorno, a Jew, says about jazz?" She didn't. He instructed her.

Things came to a head the day she told him, habituated to full disclosure with Dennis, she'd gone to "The Panther". He stared.

"The lesbian bar." Not news.

"Meet anybody nice?"

"I was just curious, that's all."

He proceeded to lecture for forty-five minutes on the virtues of fidelity, the benefits of constancy. He was loyal, why wasn't she?

He understood the damages she had endured from Dennis, had seen what was wrong in their marriage right off, Dennis's simmering brutality, had befriended him to help him, to help *her*. To heal her. With constancy would come trust, with trust, transparency and daily ease. Together, they could achieve anything.

She interjected, "I won't be owned."

Which inspired another half hour of therapy. She was drifting into the dangerous psychological territory where lurked Jung's destructive anima. Lesbianism was a fatal form of narcissism. There had never been a happy lesbian. Just look at Janet who had started her on this dangerous path.** Estrogen to estrogen transfer caused cancer, too. ("What?") He knew her soul, could cure her. She had only to accept his care, his voice not unpleasant, light and precise except for a sight lisp lengthening a double "s" and in this case, the "les" of lesbian. He waved his hand again, a fly had entered the argument.

The next morning, she decided to limit their relation. She wouldn't, couldn't do it abruptly or absolutely. He didn't deserve that and she still felt an attachment and problematic gratitude for his solace at the breakup with Dennis. She could cut down the sex to once very two weeks, for starters. She'd spend more time at the history department library where he had no admittance, go to more evening lectures; the Buddhist studies people had all kinds of interesting offerings. And she really should visit her divorced mother in Fairfax more frequently.

So she drove up the weekend of Sept. 22 and Guy went to see his good friend Dennis, ending up making a better friend of Janet. There had been no perjury in his paean to fidelity a month earlier even if he continued to hector Karen with parts of it at any opportunity. Because Janet didn't contaminate his deep allegiance to Karen. Indeed he was sure he'd give up Janet's trafficked Love Canal in a minute if Karen asked him to. As the weeks rolled on, and he saw more (er, a lot more) of Janet than Karen, he thought to divulge all so he could definitely demonstrate where his heart was. Of course he didn't. He could never hurt her like that.

*Where did his anti-semitism come from? Where does it ever come from? His father spoke approvingly of the old country. That's not it. He read Mein Kampf and it made sense, kinda to a twelve year old who spent hours playing Risk, Stratego and Eastern Front in solo player mode. But that's not it. The intellectual Jewish kids at school who might have been his allies were clannish and took no notice of him but that's not it. He had one of those impossibly intense sixteen year old crushes on a girl who had a crush on the tennis team captain shoo-in for valedictorian and that guy was yeah you know already. Which is getting warmer. Yes, and having been bullied, he was much affected by images of Palestinian olive groves, pity pity the trees, being bulldozed on the West Bank and Gaza. Our prime suspected epidemiological vector, remains: envy. He envied lots of people in the arts and the academy and they had nothing in common except some of them had one thing in common. Why do we hate without cause? Well, why do we love without a cause? Reverse engineering the answer to that one won't yield a solution but will give a direction to probe.

**Karen had asked herself, why, given her inclinations, she had curtailed her erotic involvement with Janet despite its physical viability and the rush of comeuppance she got from making Dennis share his prize. Which led her to the answer; she had never forgiven Janet's too casual destruction of her marriage and she never would. Not in this life.

His Hospitality

Despite the new arrangement in his life, Guy saw no reason to stop his usual bi-weekly hostings of Dennis and Janet as couple, having them over for TV, *American Masters, Masterpiece Theatre* or *Live at Lincoln Center*.(Intellectuals didn't have TVs unless you were an artist who fell asleep to the colors, watching Johnny Carson with the sound off.) Indeed, there was every reason to continue, for cover's sake (a negative) and especially for the added dimension of delectation (a big positive). For *interest*, nothing beat seeing the happy pair hold hands, or heads dovelike together, chatting in couplese, Dennis possessively putting his arm around her shoulder, knowing that in just a few hours … it was delicious, it was rich. Which could not be said of Guy's bank account where the deficit at the end of the month was assuming alarming proportions, meaning he, of all people, had to think about it. Costs were high: rent, food, other basics, the gas guzzling Cutlass, tuition, the fancy art books and art supplies. His generous, guilty-they-had-given-life parents were finally grousing, asking why he never tried to sell his own art and stubbornly weren't convinced by his honest answer. Which was: It was too soon to reveal his embodied visual theories into a world that would only understand enough *to copy them*. Meanwhile, Dennis would be good for a twenty, repaid in a week, then for a fifty, not repaid, one more in the cycle of his lengthening account. Okay, he needed to economize.

Start with wine. The good stuff was wasted on Dennis who would gulp down anything with relish. Janet, a very discrete drinker, refused to appreciate the fine points of nose, blush and savor, despite some serious instruction. In other words, that was two-three quality bottles a week down the drain. Guy didn't even have to think about the solution.

Save a few empty bottles of Schist, Mouton and Chateau Gunod. Purchase one twenty-five cent funnel and one $6.98 gallon bottle of Gallo or Christian Brothers or Inglenook, nothing so low as Boones. Give bottle of vintage a new life, give plonk a new dignified identify. Place rebottlement in frig. Serve with first story: opened last night for small night cap, not ideal for fine wine but fine wine could take it, now would you like another glass, Dennis, Janet, No? Nothing discreditable about the second or third story either, they were pure art, making something of nothing which compensated Guy for the fact that he was drinking the cheap stuff too.

Guy: Did you detect that raspberry undertone?

Dennis. Ah. Well, maybe.

Guy. Do this. Sip and hold it in the back of your mouth, count to five. Raspberry.

Dennis. Oh yeah. Got it. Super.

Two nights later, different aristo label, same jacquery chop their heads off steel tank swill.

Guy. Interesting. A surprising note of cherry, right at the front.

Dennis. Yeah, right up front.

Dennis was disappointingly easy to haul in. All lures failed on Janet. Guy wanted the spy-sign, the merest entre-nous recognition, casting lingering looks at her over the top of his glass. Nothing. Once when Dennis was paying particular attention to Stratas as she discussed at intermission her view of Tatiana (doomed, herioic), Guy stuck his index finger in his mouth. Janet continued to look at him with the bland uncomprehending open face of friends. She wouldn't bite. Guy tried the obvious, winking. No response except from Dennis who asked, "Your eye all right?"

Guy replied in his best piratical, "Eye is aye-aye. Just me lash."

So it was quite note worthy the night after part three of *The Golden Bowl* (Charlotte having just snagged the Prince, Amerigo d'Espresso) when Janet took a big swallow of wine and slowly circumscribed a purple extended tongue around the rim of her glass, once, twice until it voiced a hum, rising to a low whine, an almost yearning feline moan. Dennis was mouth agape.

"Jesus, what are your doing?"

"It's a party trick. I learned it in New York."

"Jesus stop, you're going to hurt yourself."

Guy proposed a toast to break the tension.

"To the Metropolitan Museum of Art."

As host, he was all the time proposing toasts: to Mozart, Monet, Manet, Mondale, to Prof van der Mule who has just agreed to supervise his thesis. That was just the M's. And Dennis who wanted to courteously counter pledge with Mendelssohn, Mahler and Mandelstam stopped himself because Guy was "sensitive". Mondrian and James Merrill probably wouldn't do either. He contented himself with a gladiatorial arm raise of glass, carefully clinking Janet's as it descended.

'To Friends. To Friendship.'

To friends, to friendship; there were a lot of toasts.

Resolutions and Reenactments

Whatever was to happen now, Dennis needed time. It was a simple matter to call work on Monday and tell Rose the all knowing (yes, she knew) secretary that his mother was suddenly seriously ill and he needed to take the next bus to Norfolk and would she, as a special favor, tell Janet when she came in that he hoped to be back by the end of the week and would call before that. Janet wouldn't like that but the plausibility of details and her reaction no longer concerned him. He ran down to the 7/11 at night, bought beer, sweet rolls, caned tuna, orange cheese in a bizarre stocking up that seemed unreal, supplies to last him as he went underground as he called it in his rooms in the basement of the insurance manager's home. He needed to think even as the pain washed over him in waves with nauseating peaks and troughs, he'd kill her, he'd forgive her. The fount of his anger changed, it wasn't the sex, who cared how many times after the first (yet he kept estimating the times and was tortured by the thought that somewhere Guy had hash marked a score) it was their deceit, how they had controlled the situation, how they must have reveled in their knowledge, his utter ignorance being the stump around which they played erotic peek-a-boo. (Had they pitied him? Sickening.) He saw his best revenge was not to open it to the air of discovery where action would melt away like tomb paintings exposed to light. No, he would subdue them simply by being silent. Now he knew and they wouldn't know he knew and that would be his first and most effortless vengeance. He would laugh at their everyday deceits (such poker faces!) now so utterly obvious. He relished in frantic fantasizes the prospect of disrupting them in the act – he'd head over to her place at midnight, knock loudly, let Guy run out the back or hide in one of her closets for that matter. He'd invent contagious illnesses that he needed to be checked for and bug Guy as he never had about the several hundred dollars he had borrowed. He'd attack them on every front except the frontal. Meantime he'd get a car purportedly to visit his ailing mother while actually driving to DC for the bars. Why stop fucking Janet now that it was honest fucking; she was good in bed and it would have a new tang. It was bitter, bitter that he had trusted her but the phrase popped into his mind one night as he paced the linoleum tiles, "valid Appearance and real Reality", a thing Prof. Carson harped on. At the level of the phenomenon and personality he had been totally fooled, completely duped. For how long, he could guess from minor signs, for instance — when had Rose first smiled at him in an over-bright way? At least a year. At a deeper reality, the noumenal, hadn't he known, seen with complete clarity she wasn't to be trusted that night of the party, her and Rafer, the way she skipped off, too animal in her case? He'd begun with her, gone on with her because this was his destiny, she was his teacher. It was a philosophical comfort, a small sea worthy boat riding the black swells of pain. Sometimes he was on board. Yeah, it was pretty funny.

In fact, he couldn't play it cool or wait it out. What he wanted to consider was a conscious decision to do the obvious thing and just confront her had nothing to do with volition. The bottled-up knowledge was simply killing him.

He was going to be calm and measured, cool. "I know about you and Guy." She didn't blink an eyelid, her voice even, natural without a grain of strain.

"Know about what?"

Right then he lost all composure, abusing her, shouting. There was nothing to be read in her face, always pale, except its extension in a looking look, not a flicker in her composure. His righteous rage was mitigated by one thing, a reflux of cowardliness caused by a little neutral man in his head who observed that since the basement was almost perfectly sound proofed, she was completely in his power.

"How did you find out?"

"I'll ask the questions, you answer them."

More abuse. He demanded the common details, when begun, how often, how logistically arranged, places, times, what they did. She answered evenly, gravely, as if describing a thing witnessed, nothing to do with her.

"What else do you want to know? I will try to tell you. You keep asking 'why.' It began as … an accident, I told you, the night of the games. You weren't there. And then it happened. I've told you how. When it was done, I'd done it. Betrayed you. I honesty didn't see how it was much worse to continue. Yes, I liked the sex. Don't get mad. He was different than you, not better. I enjoyed having you both. I liked the victory over Karen, having her man, both her men. And yes, because of the way you treated me. As accessory."

Dennis braced to object; she held up her hand. "Please let me finish. I didn't want to lie. You can say I totally betrayed you. But I want you to know, I never verbally lied to you." She had to wait until he his violence subsided, his fist thrust close to her face becoming a finger point.

"Verbally!"

"I never consciously wanted to hurt you, though I dare say" … she stopped. "I enjoyed the game, being desired. Deciding when which of you could have me. Being bad. The drama. I never loved him. He was funny … he was a laugh."

He interjected "You didn't love him? You think that makes it better? I loved you!"

She had been looking at him directly yet her focus narrowed, she framed him in.

"You liked me, admired me, wanted me. I don't think you loved me. You didn't know me, how I would take a hurt. What I was capable of." She paused. "Now you know."

He threw it back to her ... "You never loved me."

"You know, there are people that can't love. Something wrong with them, at birth or later, something happened to them." For the first time, she was unsettled, raising both her hands. Her jaw suddenly clinched and still she spoke. "I never felt, I didn't feel ..." and she shook her head empathically, saying No, No, No, No, at each syllable he saw her teetering between dejection and control. "I don't ask for your pity." He had nothing to say about pity; pity had not yet occurred to him.

"I deserve to die. Are you going to kill me?" Her slight smile was beautiful and alien. He had seen it, where, where ... Greek kore.

For days, he had hated her in the abstract. Now that she was before him, physically if not quite humanly, he knew it was time to decide. To tell her to leave and never see her again. To tell her to leave but make no final decision. Or throw her on the bed and (re) claim her.

None of this voided an alternative. He could ask Karen if they could rebuild their lives, together. For despite the papers filed at the courthouse and the $200 divorce, she was his only wife. Who would answer, yes, no, or let time tell.

———————

Alternatively, Janet and Guy now had to face the issue: was there anything, aside from fun and games, between them? Something they now could, now had to confront. They were odd types, she of extreme beauty, he of uncommon uncouthness and in the span of that polarity stretched a possibility.

After a record making week with Janet of two consummatious evenings and one humid afternoon, it was most unpleasant to get an almost illegible letter from Dennis (mailed the day he confronted her), full of nasty accusations and a warning not to enter his physical zone. Guy knew he had to contact Janet (she had no phone) but first thing he did was to call off work for the night and go to the shooting range behind Albemarle Arms for some defensive pistol practice. It had become an interesting chess problem. The other king had finally stirred on the small board; the crucial piece was still the black queen. He didn't have a lot in common with her and hadn't she been a bit aloof lately, afterwards? Prominent in her repertory of moves, duplicity in any direction. What really bothered him was that Dennis was sure to tell Karen she had been betrayed which simply or complexly wasn't true. Shruggingly, he regretted too the loss of Dennis despite its possibly enabling a new era of logistical conveniencing once the period of active menace was over. He'd put a lot into him, intellectually speaking and Dennis would never complete his book that acknowledged his mentor, not that the detraction to civilization was likely to be much. Oh, he was demanding a check in immediate repayment of the $650 he was owed. That was another call, to mother, for fast cash for an emergency root canal and crown done by the best man in town, Doctor, Doctor … "Eckleburg" would do.

Alternatively, Dennis waited until he could see this way through to action and bought a no brand 26 cal revolver (small for the hand, big enough for the bang) at the gun shop. His landlords, hub and wife, were big Virginia football fans who'd drive to the nearby (less than six hours driving) away games. It happened that next weekend Virginia was at Maryland. His basement apartment was large (except for the furnace/utility room, foot print of the house, after all) and perfectly situated for his plan if the owner was away. He invited Guy and Janet over, turned the gun on them, told them to strip and fuck. Things got out of hand when Guy did a remarkably credible version of a half back fake, grabbed for the gun and was shot in his good leg. Was killed; was not killed. Dennis shot Janet and wounded her, resulting in a star blaze of scar on her pretty shoulder she'd show in pathetic and fetching revealment the rest of her long life. He shot both of them, killing no wounding them and was sentenced to ten, fifteen, twenty years in Gouchland State Prison. The Commonwealth's Attorney knew he couldn't make murder stick with all that distress of mind. It was manslaughter, aggravated wounding with discharge of a fire arm within city limits as one of those prosecutorial chasers that says "this is really serious or we wouldn't even bother to pile on with the minor charge, would we?"

One day, suddenly and embarrassingly after the fact, it came to him: Karen must have felt this pain. A rough justice was at work even if too late for her to probably appreciate it. The thought of his getting more or less what he deserved only made him more desperate. He hated everything about his old life that had led him to this bitter void. A scientist was spending twelve hours a day trying to discover what was killing gays, the lady who saved gorillas has just been killed and some guy was climbing the tallest mountains to put up ozone monitors "and here I am living in a basement, writing a book no one will ever read, crying over the common treachery of a pretty face." A week after this revelation, Dennis walked briskly down the highway (the same road where he and Karen had first talked with Guy) to the shopping center to a small storefront, "Armed Forces Careers" between the post office and Walmart, entered the Navy recruiting door and joined up. What was two years? Nothing compared to the time he had been in a prison of lies. It was the most different thing he could imagine from his current life and he'd always liked the idea of being in uniform and doing your duty. The recruiter was professionally friendly, glib and sharp eyed, going through all the options so Dennis couldn't focus on any one, adding at the end, "You know the beard goes. This is the *American Navy*". Two weeks later, he was at Chicago, Lake Station for basic training. Which was, as he anticipated, worse than he had imagined, the always barked commands, the ridiculous regimes (never call a petty officer "Sir", never step over the blue line, always salute the left of the entry door (the barracks being an honorary ship with an imaginary flag on the stern), being awakened the middle of the night for push-ups, the hosings down, the mindless drills and sapped out fellow recruits. Somehow he got through it, eight weeks of misery taking him far from the searing pain of his friends' betrayal which began to seem really of no importance compared to getting up for another day of brain blanking fatigue, meaningless memorization and being yelled at. The last two weeks were better, a qualifying line had been crossed, most of the Mickey Mouse dropped away to reveal a substrata of meaning; obeying reasonable orders, being where you needed to be, wearing the regular uniform that sported its first anchor insignia. The dizzying vistas of freedom were boxed in and four walled, it was being under decks in a big boat with no worry about where it was going.

Passed as seaman second class and after a special clerical course (he wore glasses, after all) Yeoman Nelson was ordered to Central Administrative Command, Atlantic Fleet. So much for seeing the world, he was seeing the north end of Norfolk, where he'd been born. He wasn't happy, typing up officer fitness reports, leave authorizations, filing and processing a myriad of pre-desk top computer-forms. He waited for an opening at sea; applied, was transferred to Enterprise, sailed two tours to the Med. There were easy girls and quality whorehouses in the major ports, Marseilles, Naples, the Piraeus where he worked out his erotic resentments. Returning to Norfolk after his second tour, now a seaman first class and on his way to petty officer third, he met Susan, the daughter of a retired navy man who was helping out (she was helping him) at the USO enlisted man's dance. Petit, perky, dark haired, smart, she was studying for her nursing degree after graduating from Old Dominion in biology. They struck it off, he liked her life-elan, her openness and stability; she, his seriousness, tentativeness and something not quite fathomed. He really wasn't natural navy mate-rial. They married eight months later. He didn't want to lose her.

Dennis, now Petty Officer, was upon promotion transferred to the Navy Annex, DC, Junior then Senior Surface Officer

Assignments. Later, it was to the Old Navy Yard for Congressional liaison stuff. The academy graduates could talk and think. They just couldn't write. The years passed, their three children, Susan, Eve and Nathan grew up. They weren't philistines, going to museums and concerts. In 2010, after twenty-five years of service, Senior Chief Petty Officer Nelson and wife retired back to Tidewater, to a 1990s brick ranch house built on a little inlet off Lynnhaven in Virginia Beach. She still worked part-time in a local doctor's office; Dennis tended a big mixed garden of flowers and vegetables, something he had missed all those years at sea and in navy housing. He was researching a book on the Confederate Navy, encompassing the standard works (nothing like the number on Lee's army), none purely from his angle, logistics and paperwork. He knew about administration, how navies float on paper.

He never wrote another word of fiction. Preparing for the move back to Tidewater, he'd come across the old manuscript of his novel, its manila folder crumbling in his hand. The Crane's bond, with the rusted fox ear of the paper clip at the corner, oxidized off-white was very readable even if the typed letters had begun to fade. It would be a downer, he'd read it later, which he did on the first chill night in the new house. Sheets in hand, his fingers recalled grasping the tabs to set the margins wide as possible and how he always typed too close to the end of the page, making a crazy slant of lines. The people and the story meant nothing to him. It was all so literary and distant. He could appreciate something of the intensity but it was like looking through the wrong end of binoculars, the scope small compared – to what? To any day of ache and work and play and contestation and joshing camaraderie aboard the Lady Entty, the Big E, the Enterprise, to passing notes to the admiral under the camera's lights, to getting up with the babies, Nathan's first home-run, to Susan's look, face to face. He crumpled each page read and tossed them with hard throws like base balls into the fireplace, passing its first test, where they'd land or bounce on the logs, catch on the grate and briefly smolder before breaking into a blossom of flame that left a black petaled rose, tinged with orange. He felt the glow of childish glee, a deeper satisfaction. "It is finished, my book of embers."

Life was good. His eyes could follow the variably sky colored water of the inlet to the Point where, narrowing in vision, he knew it widened into the gray, the featureless sea. He had sailed that sea responsibly (even if his most durant memories were ambient; constant noise, lack of privacy, the bulkhead curtailed sightlines) and standing now in his own yard, taking in the immediate air of cut grass and the raw wood of the vegetable boxes he had made with own hands, he felt such absolute possession of his life he didn't fear anything time would bring, not even what it (Susan had seen much in the clinics) must bring.

Only very rarely Janet or someone that could only be her would come to him in dreams. Always she was silent with her characteristic look of composure, always he was trying to urgently tell her something. He would awake those mornings discomforted yet it was in the balance of his life almost nothing. He could be charitable, hope she was alive and doing okay; it was all a long time ago. Forgiveness he could see was an honest thing; you did it for yourself. (Yet he couldn't wish her happiness, since the smallest probe of thought never failed to incite the deeply vested wound.) As to Karen, they'd stayed in distant touch. She was some kind of Buddhist big wig, sending him photocopied Christmas-Buddhist New Year update letters and was always up to something. This year it had been installing computers in one of the new Tibetan nunneries outside Dharamsala, followed by a personal audience with the Dali Lama.

Lacking is the luminosity and fluency of fiction. What we have: the unburnished recordation of average days. History is banal (even at it most catastrophic), a simple weave of four common threads – he said, she said, something done or not, the coarse canvas of our lives. And always, the white mice and the black mice, gnawing.

He. That's not what happened. It was just another alternative.

She. I know. You can't play with your readers like that. It's disrespectful.

He. I don't have any readers.

She. You clearly don't want any.

He. Correct.

She. You don't know you won't have any. Somebody might find it in a drawer. Because you don't intend to destroy the manuscript do you? Write it and burn it?

He. Why would I do anything so pointless: write it and burn it?

She. So we are back where we started. You are insulting your readers or readers, your *potential* readers.

He. Not necessarily. Scale is a factor. If I were to have one to three readers, then they might, in their rarity, mean a great deal too me, less being more, so that to treat them ... I object to your insultingly and offer *dismissibly* ...

She. Quite an improvement.

He. Then to treat them, say, "offhandedly", would be a supreme compliment in that despite everything, I knew they'd see me through.

She. Ah. "Not give you up", as James puts it.

He nods.

She. Balderdash. Let me ask you some straight questions.

He. Fine.

She. You have identified Karen as woman who definitely preferred sex with women. Yet you record, all too briefly, her involvement with Guy. How does that work?

He. Consider, it was brief. I think you can see how Karen's sleeping with Guy, Dennis's best friend, would be compensation or demi-revenge for her. Furthermore, she was lonely and he was at hand and in the right sequence. Also, since this is chronicle of truth, the truth must be told. Guy had a small penis, stiff enough and tooting, about the size of a boatswain's whistle (or for the non-nautical, a breadstick). Physically, as far as Karen was concerned, he was woman. Here, a great secret is revealed (like all so called great "secrets", it is widely known if not widely published): many women prefer a sprat over a sturgeon for comfort's sake and ease of use. Janet also found a small size congenial, though she was ever adjustable about sizings. She too found Guy "feminine" and would occasionally dress him up in a blonde wig and faded, second string barter belt for added kink and festivity.

She. You have said, too many times, this is a history. I say the catalog of all-too-telling details like the wig sounds like you're making it up. History or fiction?

He. It is a fictional history, or historical fiction, with added elements of comedy and anti-pastoral. It is, in other words, a historical, anti-pastoral comedic fiction, or given that all these terms are notationally valid, describing a formal border, a satirical hysterical …

She. Stop. I get the reference and it's not as I like it. Aside from the lack of any coherent structure, what I really dislike is the random shifting of narrative stances, first person, third person, no person. You call it – "literary mixed media". It reminds me of an under funded urban zoo; lots of animals, all sad and shabby.

He. That's the kind of thing Janet would say.

She. I "got" the Janet resemblances a long time ago.

He. You're not getting *it*. Our daily mental narrative consists of first person transcripts of our own actions, third person ones of others but crucially, third person of ourselves once we are past the near past. In moments of high intensity when the frame of the "I" can't handle the load, we perceive a figure like another person, our selves going through the motions. So this medley of narrative persons is the most naturalistic style imaginable. Indeed, I have or someone quite like me has already contacted that body most appreciative of literary naturalism, the Nobel Committee, so they will know where to find "me".

She. Sure. Now tell me what really happened, starting at the end?

He. Right. Dennis decided he had to have it out with Guy. Man to man stuff. Knowing this could quickly become confrontational, and that Guy was armed with neat Italian heat (Beretta: 23 caliber short, seven shot automatic as aforesaid), he resolved to up gun him with an 8 shot Smith & Wesson 32 caliber auto. Not unexpectedly things quickly got out of hand. Guy and Dennis exchanged shots at close range (these pistols are notoriously inaccurate). Guy was wounded in the left leg (his good foot side so upon recovery his natural limp evened out.)

Dennis was initially charged with attempted murder, the usual bluff and scare 'em indictment before agreeing to a plea of attempted manslaughter (2nd degree), assault with a deadly weapon and discharge of a fire arm within the city limits. He was sentenced to six years, served four years in the Gouchland County correctional facility before his parole in 1988. While in prison, he earned a Master's degree in English literature from Harvard University's Barabbas Extension School.

She. And next thing you'll say is that he's a professor now.

He. I thought you put the questions and I provided the answers? But yes, that's right. He subsequently received his Phd in English from Harvard, palled around with Heaney in a gentler version of the Mailer-Jack Abbot dynamic and now teaches at an important southern mid-Atlantic university.

She. Will you cut the comedy? Sorry. WILL you cut the comedy? You must know that while there is no difficulty about a problematic narrative and a questioning or ironical narrator (*Pale Fire*) or even multiple narrators, this twitchy one-upmanship, facetious and farcical, not funny, undermines your whole enterprise, especially the good parts. The constant undercutting is a reverse motion that doesn't add depth, only a backfill of superficiality. It is unpleasant. Why do you do it?

He. Repudiation. If I told you to reject everything I have written and did so in beautiful prose, you'd say "How eloquent your argument against itself is against itself, this writing against writing. Do go on." If I did so in plain speaking, you'd clap me on the back and say "Things aren't so bad, buck up. We understand how it is." I act out my renunciation and abrogation, picking the scribal scab to make your skin crawl. Ask yourself, what are intentionally rebarbative texts resisting and why? Answer: the strong light of a too facile access that disinfects the only place where intricate and delicate microrganisms can thrive, the murky mix of a complex culture

She. Thanks. I prefer the clarity of cuvee Austen or even the plain plonk of John Grisham to the sour satisfactions of your cloudy vinegar, any day.

He. Why I do it? Alternatively, dementia. I am suffering from a long-term and progressive cognitive decline, marked by delusions, memory loss-fixation and compulsive obsessive verbal behaviors. The aliment is genetically based and currently, there is no cure. There is hope. Variously diagnosed as Chronolog's Disease or

She. "Old Age."

He. Correct. Now let me be very explicit. I'm a dotard, time tainted with that stale old man smell (blended with Bourbon and the rarer whiff of Wacky Bac) that even the most aromatic of bath beads cannot eradicate, living in a mildewed concrete block G.I. Bill bungalow in the Belmont section of Charlottesville, a blue collar neighborhood with high crime rates due to the NIMBY zoned pubic schools and housing. I admit all this since I do not now wish (or hope) to get communications of the type that, formerly, even if never received, motivated me to write:

"Your book sends hot and cold shivers down my aesthetic spine. Naked and in lather, I'm hoping we can meet to discuss your work."

Yours truly,

Naomi Roth, 27, graduate student

Vera Fielder, 36, Associate Professor

Kim Kim-Park. 44, Provost, the University Of Virginia.

Address all letters to:

Unapologetic Factor

Literal Trivial,

The Tin Age, U.S.A.

She. Which pointless peroration should be *The End*.

He. Not quite, *I* have a question.

She. Yes? You are going to confuse people with these personified Q's and A's.

He. Who are you? You embody aspects of Janet, her good mind and critical orientation, her independence, her ostensive moral allegiance to truth with her practice of evasion. And I think you sleep around.

She. It's my profession.

He. Oh, you admit you're a ...

She. Muse.

"The muse loves poets and blinds them so they can become makers of songs."

[Editor's Note. This final exchange inspired an intense discussion in the WRITE's seminar, Traces and Transcriptions. All twelve of the young critics in training regarded the muse attribution as the only real "false affirmation" in the work and the one most damaging in its obliquity. The seminar director took their decisively over invested stance as an opportunity for deeper literary forensics. The author's positing of an inspirational identity, which could only be evaluatively positive, had not been justified by any prior predication. As such, it was interpreted as inauthentic or as another of his intentional diversion- subversions. This proper conclusion precluded a more complex eventuality. That the author, reaching the same conclusion as valid and hence replicable, might still achieve a positive valence by assertion in confident expectation that other readers would latterly perform the identical by no means esoteric critical praxis. This reciprocal recognition, activated as a foreground/background dynamic, changes the frame of perception from one of mere predication to one that has done the "labor of the concept", premising the positive proposition. As a result of this analysis, seven of the seminar participants accepted the muse identification as attributive and non-weakening. The quotation is from the Odyssey, Book VII]

Addenda. Rhetorical Renderings

(Rendering = performances, drawings, animal waste by-products)

Closing arguments.

Against the motion.

Ladies and gentleman of this jury of the lectorate for many hours you have attended, read and mediated. The task before you today is a difficult one and I have no doubt you are up to it. It to decide individually and collectively on the emotion "do you care about the character "Dennis" as here presented. Now I've no doubt you feel a sincere human sympathy. That's right and proper. But the standard of care you are being asked to apply in approving the motion is different from that. It's a higher, may I say harder standard, with the force of law, defined in *Black's Dictionary*. There we read "care" means and I quote "empathy, a deep sympathy; feelings of support tending towards identification and, this is crucial, approval."

Now you must ask yourselves if this more extensive, legal and yet precise sense of caring is what you feel for the author.

He is a wife-beater, this by his own confession. You read his statement. Did he seem sorry? We know he struck his wife and more than once. Did he also strike Ms Nielson? She has not addressed the issue, says nothing on the matter, Yea or nay. I think you should consider that.

In his relations with Ms Nielson, I think the record shows he was callous, egoistical, selfish, in a word "careless." He expected loyalty; loyalty on his own terms but would not offer those common bonds of commitment which any woman and may I say most men, good decent, may I say "everyday" men want: marriage, a family, a shared abode. A home. In a word "respect".

He demanded his freedom and I submit he reaped the fruit of that freedom. Later, he finds he didn't like the fruit. Didn't, I dare say, care for the freedom either. I ask, ladies and gentlemen, what is the oldest morale in the book? You reap what your sow.

I do not say and you would not find that Ms Nielson acted perfectly. Most of us in this life do not. She is an attractive, vulnerable woman, subject to forces and situations not entirely of her of own choosing that never, I stress never would have come to fruition had Mr Dennis done just one thing; been more kind.

I have no doubt ladies and gentleman of *your* fundamental kindness. Or of your common sense and sense of fairness which will direct you to refuse a motion of empathy, empathy in the strong sense defined, to the appellant, this careless, self-pitying man.

Thank you.

For the Motion.

Ladies and gentlemen. My learned friend has provided you with the crucial definition in the case before you. And he is correct; your job is difficult, more difficult than he allows. For with all the matter of defining, what you are dealing with, your heavy, very human responsibility, isn't rules or definitions or neat judgments – though they all play a part but feeling, our human feelings that make us human.

In his statement, my learned friend says my client wasn't perfect and I agree with that.

He struck his wife. We know that because he confessed it. My learned friend is wrong to imply he did it often or that he felt no regret. How can he know that?

We do not excuse but we must ask, what was the cause my client's bad behavior?

Imagine you are a young man, in the full spate of manhood. You take the marriage vow seriously yet get no satisfaction in this marriage. Because your wife, cannot or will not confront, come to grips with or even admit her essential and alternative sexuality, an avoidance that gives him only the hard choice: frustration or disloyalty. For three years he chooses loyalty.

After three years he leaves his wife for Ms Nielson, a very attractive person as my learned friend puts it who I am sure, as we shall see, agrees with this his assessment.

Let there be no doubt there were commitments and pledges of loyalty in this latter relationship, perhaps not exactly as we would have then, but real ones, vowed by both parties, respected by one.

Ms Nielson, we are not surprised to learn, is a very cool and competent character who can manage her intrigues *almost* perfectly. Two years into his relationship with her, my client learns that she is having an affair already of one year's duration and that her lover is – his best friend. Now I don't have much to say about that party except may we all be spared such "best" friends. However condemnable, in a sense, he too is a dupe, the seduced. Have no doubt that it is Ms Nielson who is calling the shots, enjoying every act of the tawdry drama in which she is the star.

Ladies and gentlemen, we are adults, we have all suffered loss and most of us some defeat in this battle of life. Because we have this hard won knowledge, we recognize the lineaments of distress in others, we not only respond to the cries of those in pain, we observe and we understand. Looking at this case and my client's unfortunate position, I believe, on the basis of what you know and feel, you will endorse the motion of empathy. And let me, say contrary to my learned friend, this has nothing to do with "approval" or does so only in your recognition that life is path, often a hard one. We learn, so help us God; this man [gestures to the appellant] learned – and no one died.

I hope this be will will be sufficient for you to affirm the motion, that you will spare yourselves the more intense interrogation of trying to identify with my client, get inside his head, be in his skin, situate yourself in the terrible place where through the red haze of pain, he sees what his friends are and who he is.

Excerpt from The Official History: Vol. 3. Operations Around the Quotidian Depression:

Reverse at Pride's Point and "The Stand"

The forces of Fidelity, consisting of three untested battalions of Norfolks and a regiment each of eight inch artillery and tanks were aligned along the spine of Pride's Point which joined the Ego Plateau on the west and fell off preiciptatiously in the east, a posture valuable for anchoring a further advance but as events were to show, potentially disastrous if attack came suddenly from an unlooked for quarter when neither the infantry or the detached armor, intending to assume a hull down defense, had taken time to dig in the hard moraine.

Panzers of Von Lothario's Opportunist "Kampf Gruppe Manstch", advancing quietly on rubber stifflers, with captured "friendly" vehicles in the van, easily penetrated the western perimeter at dusk and were ideally positioned for a full attack as night fell.

Out posts of the Norfolks were slow to respond to the threat and quickly overrun. The main force responded, if it were possible, even less creditably. There was consternation, confusion and near chaos as a lack of combat experience (or realistic battle drill) and overconfidence in what was perceived as an unassailable defensive formation bore bitter and predictable fruit. Despite scattered instances of resistance, Lothario's forces easily routed the stunned possessors of the Point. Losses already significant, all the armor being too forward for a coherent response, mounted as near panicked defenders fled down the Point's ravines. Nor was there respite for those that reached the plain as Opportunists aimed down from the heights, though this fire was untargeted and relatively ineffectual in the darkness. Around 11 PM, Lothario gave the order to logger for the night. In less than four hours, his forces had pushed the defenders off an essential tactical objective, at minimal cost. It was, by any measure, a fine victory.

Nonetheless, the rapid advance had disorganized his echelons and ammunition was low. It was a reasonable decision to halt, re-supply, reorder and rest his men for what was expected to be a rapid and devastating pursuit of the reeling and dispirited Fidelists at first light. A price might be paid if not being prepared for a night advance off the ridge, they were too quick on the morrow and things were not as they gave every indication of being.

Defiling down the ridge, the Opportunist infantry would be exposed at sunrise to fire, being illuminated themselves before anything could be distinguished on the darkling plain. Which wouldn't matter if it was as believed they were in pursuit of a scattered and indeed shattered force.

In fact, the Fidelists had retreated in confusion but with arms. The three headquarters units, thrown together, coalesced, cooperating more effectively in the crisis than they ever had in success. They perceived a chance. *If* they could form a line of defense, requiring nothing more than rifle pits, they might at first light, catch the Os coming down ridge. They would need to hold their fire until enough of the enemy were deployed to disrupt a significant formation and cause meaningful damage before too many had fanned out to overwhelm and out flank the less numerous defenders. The rifle pits would have to be close to the anticipated line of contact so that artillery on the heights had no clear identification of friend or foe, preventing supporting fire, thus obviating the Opportunists advantage in heavy weapons. Distance, timing and a hitherto not manifested discipline would be everything.

In war more than in life, nothing is perfect. Some elements in the line began a premature fusillade that fortunately for the Fs was interpreted as desultory shots from a dissolving rear guard. A half hour later, over thirty-five hundred Lee Enfields opened up in short range, rapid fire mode on the slowly fanning out Os, the effect like one hundred machine guns, more lethal for being more broadly sited and so harder to suppress. Surprised and without cover, O casualties were immediate and heavy. Thus began the famous "Stand." The outcome of the larger action would turn on which side was first reinforced. Time was nominally on the Opportunist side, still the strong force in the battle frame, with tanks, especially the short four inch gunned "bread stick" infantry killers, moving along the long shoulders of the Ego plateau, debouching to attack on both flanks.

Reinforcements for the Fs were already in route from Port Said through the Allah Ghorai Depression, with orders to come on at maximum speed. Meantime, the ad hoc but coalesced force of infantry, artillery men, command and logistical staffs showed no sign of breaking. Their mission was conceptually and morally simple: to do what they knew they should have the night before: fight and hold on. If both sides were reinforced simultaneously, the stage was set for a decisive battle.

Popular writers at the time (and later) have referred to "The Miracle of the Stand." That the Fs were able to turn and fight despite the severe reverse of Sept 18th was due less to command "grip" than to emergent regimental pride and latent habits of good soldering. One would be wrong to facilely call these things "miraculous" though upon a deeper contemplation of how human beings function unexpectedly and sometimes exceptionally in crises, perhaps they are.

Bits

The following section includes selections from my prior collections (*Zen and Tonic, Dicta and Contradicta, A Wilderness of Monkeys* and *Trooping the Colour),* along with new material. To say it braces the nave of narrative would appear counterfactual since the relationship of nave to buttress in cathedrals is a structurally organic one, each supporting the other. This disconnect is only apparent, in two dimensions of arrangement and apprehension. In the subterranean third dimension of art, where all creation happens, paralipomena and story are linked in an arch of stress and countervailing pressures.

[Editor's note. There is no content from the last two titles, the only existent ones, in the current volume. Nelson's antic mendacities are the subject of a forthcoming note in Parenthesis, the student edited journal of the William Ruminant Institute of Textual and Editorial Studies (WRITES). See www.parenthesis@ WRITES.org.]

After visiting my doctor, I am always resolved to live more fully and forcefully. This is a routine of my reliably boring life.

We shouldn't find it curious that some Death Row prisoners are obsessed with sex. And we are all sentenced to death.

The betrayed lover who forgives is saying "no one could love you more than this." The "guilty" party has, almost generously, placed the "innocent" in this superior position; possibly, I do not say it is likely, the sometime point of the entire melodrama.

What's annoying about every religion is that on the fundamental issues of life/death, right / wrong and what is meaningful action, they have stopped asking questions and are confidently providing answers.

The congested world doesn't need another person or another book. But if you find yourself alive you might as well scribble since, requiring minimal maintenance, the good enough book obtains without much difficulty a low redemptory orbit that drags the author along – that of being *less* less needed.

Two book dedications I could approve of: "To whom it may concern" and "You and love are still my argument" will, by AD 2115, require for comprehension a dissertation's worth of gloss.

To have no interest in pleasing anyone is evidence of uniqueness of vision. Pleasing even one demonstrates a sad decline in singularity.

If forceful enough and varied, criticism has the effect of hammering one into an unassailable position that's perfect for hazarding the next advance.

The aphorism is so intensely verbal, one flees with relief to reading (or writing) a three hundred page novel.

Thought's first strike into words is in the coinage of the aphoristic slug. All literature from Charlie the Tuna to "chariots of fire" is crafted from this core ore. Of limited receptive capacity, we are intrigue-fatigued by its developmental suggestibilities and perforce have to take it slow.

The accurate aphorism hits the subject's bull's eyes, yes and that is the problem, missing the wider circlets of coverage.

"Good things from the garden / garden in the valley/ valley of the jolly, Ho, Ho,Ho,/ Green Giant." Fifty thousand poets, working over five decades, have crafted no lyric that surpasses it.

Since in a hundred years at current rates of progress no one will be reading anything except technical articles, the aphorism is positioned as a defensive foxhole along the long retreat of language.

To guarantee urban and personal renewal, build on unreliable foundations. (from *Zen and Tonic*)

Black hole. At the apogee of one's freedom, to feel even then its attractive power, having acquired a taste for strange physics.

Native advice: to certain Amazonian tribesmen: stop beating your heads with big sticks even if it's a sociable way of settling disputes; it's bad for your brains. To certain writers: stop dumbing yourselves down even if it's a reasonable way of getting an audience; it's bad for your work. And probably your brains.

Your friends won't tell you truths that hurt you and your enemies won't tell you ones that help. They are the same truths, the ones you must need to know.

Sadness of the serial killer; hoping it was the last time and knowing, like masturbation, it isn't.

There's magic in the alchemy of converting pain to art even if the resulting object isn't gold but a lump of shapened lead.

The two horses harnessed to the chariot of achievement are "Ambition" and "Disappointment". If hardly ever pulling together, one will generally follow the other.

The room of your life is penetrated by the horror. You wall it off and have two rooms. Your intelligence can't cope with the duplex, its painful furnishings so in that relation you become stupid. Now that you are stupid *and* intelligent, are you wiser? Your being, no longer contiguous, is compartmentalized, complicated. Is it more interesting, more capacious?

The common vehicle of remembered pain conveys us to the past with force, vivacity and detail. More real than real, it's like time travel except for the venues being limited and that the action "real" (fictional) time travelers are able to do and told not to do lest they annihilate themselves is the one thing we keep trying to do – change the past if only to rid our selves of our transporting device.

That some people thinking you were great gave you awards, prizes and grants when you weren't says nothing about your work but a lot about some people, their prizes, awards and grants.

Buddhist lamas are justly revered as masters of high esoterica, experts in extreme mental development. Nothing indicates they would be especially good at managing the desires and careful responsibilities of the average person.

After humanity, rats are predicted to be next top species. Being mammals, one can predict the evolution of their art: rat naturalism, rat expressionism, rat abstraction, Rationalism, etc. For real novelty, we'll have to wait for the rise of the Insecta in three million years when not a single human artifact remains. Such clearances! Yet human art that needs no appreciators to exist may require no physical carrier to survive, achieving an eternal registration via a comprehensive aesthetic "mathematics" we cannot as embodied beings directly access. This is mystical, what's merely over the limit of the known. The impossible is another thing entirely.

Few things have become more tiresome than the critic who cobbles together insights from brain science (the brain operates in sections, the brain filters reality, etc.) and Buddhism (the self is not the sum of the parts OR any one part) to conclude identity and ego are illusions. What if identity is a natural construct, a tool? Then the issue isn't reality versus delusion but usefulness. Is the tool well used or not and for what ends?

In strictly natural terms, individuals are useless except as carriers of DNA. Individuals are also carriers and creators of culture. Art, at conception, is always individual; to this extent Nature endorses the particular person with his/her temporary freight of ego.

If we could escape Death by eschewing Sex, all of us would sign on. And nearly all of us would violate the contract even at the penalty of Death.

Sex is the dream of life. We sometimes listen to children and the old because they are awake in ways the prime time adults never are.

Music Lessons

Wagner: the most exquisite musical sensitivity in the service of thematic crudity, a vibrating contradiction along the same line as sex which is intimate and impersonal, delicate and vulgar.

Our appetite for intensity is much greater than our capacity to absorb it. Schubert.

In every stave of his music, Schumann expresses (exhibits) his reverence for human nobility, beauty, purpose and love. Clearly a lunatic.

Having first agreed that most of Mozart is elevator music that lacked a lift, we can proceed to have a productive conversation about music. K 375 is indicative, musical farts rumbling through an acoustic gut. {Contradictum: "Can't you see that criticizing in these terms one of the greatest creators in our culture exposes you as small and mean minded?" Irony conceals satisfaction. May not contempt convey respect?}

Personal Prejudice. After Hitler, there is no excuse, cover, expiation therapeutic or social for anti-Semitism so the feeling of rage, no different from hatred, one has upon encountering it should perhaps only be tempered by the thought that in the extremity of that moment one is most like the anti-Semite.

One shouldn't judge a philosophy by the physiognomy of its deviser but in a world of many deep thinkers and limited time, one look at Heidegger's smug yet guilty puss was enough to persuade me to take a pass. True, Hannah Arendt found him congenial; some good woman is always willing to give some bastard a redemptory benefit of the doubt by opening her mind and body. Alright, I did seriously try to read him, found him incomprehensible ("The Nothing nothings, the World worlds.") and was advised "He does make sense … in German." Fine. Note: every other German philosopher has the good sense to make sense in our ever accommodating, "feminine" English.

That Germany, one of the most cultivated nations in Europe and Japan, the most aesthetic culture on earth, both went so wrong politically suggests a disinvestment of intelligent away from beauty in favor of crassness and practicality (i.e. the United States) may have unexpected societal benefits. (Put another way: the aesthization of politics is usually fatal.)

The panzer division properly laagered its tanks during the worst of the Russian snows only to find they wouldn't start up in the spring. Mice had entered through gaps in the steel no wider than a penny to eat the insulation off the wiring. There are complex lessons here about conflicting agendas and how one party's ends becomes another's means. The main point is to never underestimate mice in their drive to eat, reproduce and have a nice house.

In this respect, they are much like us only more single minded and thus very worthy opponents. As is often the case with formidable antagonists, it may be necessary to fight unfairly to beat them which is not to justify applications of cruelty and contempt that are, moreover, morally self-subverting. Please, no glue traps.

In writers' school, one of the imperative instructions is "kill your beauties". Why would you do that? In the interest of a higher beauty. After all, they aren't real beauties, they are stylistic vanities. Makes sense but I'm not killing mine. They have the hard charm of a Kirchner street walker. They're all I've got. Nor can I rid myself of the suspicion that the guy who advises "kill your beauties" is pimping his.

I have studied systems – Kant's, Hegel's, the tantras as deeply as anyone.* They seem to me beautiful rugs, plush, intricate, all nailed down that cover a lot of ground. I prefer the little mat that's prone to slippage and in that instant most like a flying carpet. Some of my observations could, with difficulty, be systematically stitched together. All could easily be organized. I leave them as they fall, throw(n) rugs in the hope they will trip you up.

(* A boast, a rhetorical trope. I have studied them as deeply as *I* could, at best a shallow depth, the middling dimension of freedom.)

The pace of technological change is so fast and the pace of writing so slow, all "creative writing" is now historical fiction.

The betrayed, having been doubly generous, first by providing the necessary condition for the transgressors' diversion, then upon discovery, stimulating them to the gratification of their regret-reformation (for of course, the perpetrators meant no harm) are justly aggrieved, getting nothing from the transaction except the comfortless satisfaction of being "right" and a knowledge they did not want.

"Knowledge you do not want." The only real kind, everything else is mere information.

Lament, somebody said, is always learning. [Editor's note: "Nur die Klage lernt noch.", Rilke, Sonnets to Orpheus, no.8.]

Having critically appreciated the work of my teachers, I am ahead of them. Except that they must already be beyond their last work (where I am) and allied with time, are still in front. Unless they aren't, having already fallen from their never secured crest to leave me in possession of a slope where to advance is to go downhill.

A Fine Whine. We all know that forgiving those that betray you is wrong; it's too easy, they've been let off the hook. It can't be good for their character which is the best reason to forgive them. At all cost they must be denied the dignity and high ground of "victim", specifically being the target of your revenge, an always instant satisfaction that deferred acquires tints and tastes, the complex of savors that enhance and characterize the superior appreciations of a refined person.

The platitudinous statement "art must give pleasure" is non controversial provided it is conceded the pleasure doesn't have to be pleasurable. Art is like sex; the point isn't pleasure per se but gratification.

Pleasure cannot be the index of art because The Three Stooges can give more pleasure than Sophocles. The Beach Boys are more life encouraging than Bach. Great art is discomforting, transporting us to places high and low we don't want to go, it challenges our contented complacencies. Everyone knows creative consciousness is unhappy and everybody is wrong. That many artists have been happy in their persona lives and in the practice of their art doesn't falsify the fact that their best work springs from some dissatisfaction, the relationship of the artist to his art being metaphorically sadomasochistic just as that of the true appreciator to the object is approach-avoidance, love-hate.

Few things are easier than talking nonsense about art and numerous careers have been based on nothing else.

Instant, inconsistent, arbitrary and variable, the rules children make up for their games are only meaningful as regulators of the game. This describes the human condition.

The problem with aphorisms as a genre is the same as paintings in museums – there too many of them, all openly positioned, belonging to no one. What inspires and deepens attention is the single item solely possessed; an average seascape over a neighbor's mantel, a book on loan from a friend with one sentence of urgent underlining you must search for.

Driving and constantly shifting, in time the gears became the wheels and shifting them the terrain. (from *Zen and Tonic*)

Since what would make me doubt the value of my artistic efforts is approval, I've undermined them with any number of self subter-fuges, stunts and shticks which also allows me the flattery of think-ing how excellent my work would be without them. Naturally, I'd be chuffed if those were the very elements that were admired and I'm not the kind of person to lie about that (trust me!) even if this thought begins to acquire all the characteristic wiggles of a fresh red herring, "underwriting" in the insurance sense.

Keats — "Poetry should come as naturally as leaves on trees." *Naturally* does not mean *easily*. In spring, trees groan with the labor of their forthcoming green.

Shelving in the library. So many thousands of books. I think "facile writing flows from facile thoughts, hard to do writing from complex thoughts" only to hear the laughter, not of Aphrodite but of Athena.

A certain class of victim has this solace. "Getting involved with a murderer, an embezzler, a liar, what was I asking for but murder, fraud and lies?"

The real humiliation of being betrayed isn't that you were appraised below the estimation of what you thought was your contracted worth but that the betrayer returns from his excursion in bright apologetic expectation that what was so easily put at stake, yourself, will now be returned with interest. These are the ultimate confi-dence men (and women) of a type that the devalued faithful, to spite themselves, are inclined to appreciate, thinking , "I must be of some value that he/she took such trouble to injury me."

That is, they have sized you up and determined you are *not* worthy of the most basic human respect, honesty in dealing. What a novel idea – this never occurred to you – and of incontestable validity because nothing in the moral order stopped it from happening. Your sense of dignity and self-worth were, who knew, *conceits*. Be grateful to your teachers. In other words: *He had build the usual fortifications: deep entrenchments, decoy selves, small detachments that went back and forth in routines that looked like armies, instruments that could detect assaults from far off, weapons to fight back, proud banners hung on the battlements. When the attack got through (always there is the undefended stretch, the weakness in the wall, the traitor, the underminer), after everything was pillaged and he was totality exposed in the ruins of his bastions which were the limbs of his nakedness, it was then he almost got it – a glimpse of himself.*

It would be wrong to make too much of a fuss about any of it. Only let's be clear about the issues. It's not about the ulcerations of an illusionary ego, the impermanence of human arrangements, or even (op cit.) waking up to reality. It's about every being's expectation that it will be the object of correct action and every being's (even an ant's) disappointment when it isn't.

Camus says "Doubts are the most intimate things about us." This is humane. I say pride is the most intimate thing about us. There's always the weak point where our bright armor links up with ego and that is where the dagger strikes. Nothing is more intimate than a wound. Which becomes a kind of armor; one is impervious to all shorter stabs.

We could live a million years and the most fundamental question would still be what to do with our lives? Death is life-enhancing by encouraging us to solve the problem within an experimentally realistic time span. Perspective generated by the vanishing point.

Since much of what we consider "intelligence" is rapid mental energy, it sets the speed of our definitional noose. High intellect that is sluggish escapes it entirely.

Tip for writers. It was only after I took up painting that I understood the superficialities of my expositions. I could *see* them.

For all the philosophical logic chopping (brain events are not strictly identical with thoughts) it's obvious to modern people that we are our bodies and particularly, our brains. Yet an instinct speaks: as humans, we may be insufficiently equipped to fully understand our deepest nature, what we are. The brain/body thesis is too pat, as is the answer of prior centuries, we are nonmaterial souls. It is likely the real answer surpasses all our categories of spiritual/physical and function/identity. We are stranger than we can possibly know which does not exclude our being simpler than we can admit.

Let's be frank. We no longer have time to take great big boring books seriously, *Doctor Faustus, Death of Virgil, You Can't Go Home Again* and a thousand others. Playing Pac man or watching an on-screen animation of colors and shapes generated by your blood pressure/ heart rate is more gratifying and better for you especially if it lowers your blood pressure.

It is said that the foundation of civilization is the incest prohibition. Given the flaws of civilization (ones that inspire tenure secured anthropologists to declare "there is no progress"), would a society based on mother/son, father/daughter sex be worth trying? (I doubt it but you should always question your foundations). Does the incest barrier make people mean?

Irremediable from the past, injury and defeat; I still live. Irremediable from the future, Death; yet I live. What is this present "I" – a thing pulverized, pluralized, hard to kill.

In Marlowe's plays, the poetry is expansive, the drama is cramped. See young Shakespeare, wide eye and whey-faced, taking it all in.

A message from William, my broker at Stratford Properties in an up-market mode: "Even in the eyes of death, I see life appearing."

Another message: "Fixed stars govern a life." Yes Sylvia, you are right.

It is not so much Nietzsche's "what doesn't break us, makes us" as what impedes, speeds us.

Persons who late in life discover that "the great love of their life" was just a means for living should temper their disappointment with the satisfaction that they have received every benefit the system has to offer: life enhancing fiction, many years, ultimate truth.

English "doesn't like" bald or strong assertions and perceptions; it always wants to qualify them; its "personal" manner is that of the attentive (no language listens better), rather anxious if agreeable person who says thing like "I'm sure I think I agree with what I believe you are proposing if I am hearing you correctly". The problem is that English is in a state of avoidance, it can't face the bloody trauma of Hastings and centuries of linguistic rape, it needs to temporize. Which makes it the perfect medium for Shakespeare, the Great Equivocator, whose work (strong assertion) is the greatest achievement of mankind.

Desert Island book

Captain Dreyfus, sentenced to Devil's Island to die from its brutal climate and harsh penal regimes, was allowed one book that he studied daily when he was fit enough to read. Shakespeare, in English.

Drive the stake into the heartwood and the bole may yet mend around the injury, meld about the rod so that even if by metallic conduction the tree is seared by heat and haunted by cold, it would not change being the hard-hybrid it has become. This is a parable.

You know things are going to be alright when the king, having leered into the abyss, looks up to say "Let copulation thrive, I need more soldiers."

Perpetrators jaunt along the line of time, like old Nazis hiking in the post–war Alpines. "Ja, Ja, Germany in the 1930's, 1940's crazy times, it was all a long time ago." Victims abide on a chronological chart, continuously situated at various *present* distances from its central feature, the active wound with attractive power and dimensions big enough to engulf.

Let us not be too cynical, in the literary way about humanity. Most persons have never done another human being deliberate harm. (Generally speaking, we are worst to our selves than to others. Which is a truism and truisms should not be easily credited, including this one.) That all have done harm, accidentally, unconsciously, from ignorance and mundane pain is a cause for pity not disdain.

Youth is utterly estranged by sex, the world is disordered by desire, we do crazy things, there is no rest. By age fifty, the rage lessens and we begin to feel with an equanimous clarity, the irony being we have grown so used to distortion as reality we repine our new found temperance.

The "change" in a man: when what was the little dictator of his body just lolls around, a private waiting for orders.

At about age thirty, I had lots of friends and they were easily classifiable: best friends, good friends, casual friends, formal friends (certain professors), distant and nearby friends, ones who were easy, others that were "difficult", friends I depended upon, others that depended on me, ones I'd give my live for, friends I wouldn't miss. Three decades later, some have died, others grown strangely silent, some I've offended, some have offended , some moved away, some moved down the street and suddenly there's nothing to say; others lost from politics or games (chess), relationships ended from bad advice or perceived lack of sympathy, some bored, others boring, a few too successful for taste. Some changed too little, others too much, some didn't like my partner or me theirs or the partners disliked the friend, the partner; some not in their right minds, all lost. In this regard, ending my life as I began it, there is the genuine relief of not disconsoling a single friend.

Corrida. In the ring, the bull receives an excellent education. Pity he's killed by degrees and can't use it.

Ani Tenzin Palmo asserts that when we mediate, it is not that we are pretending to be Asoka Buddha rather that Buddha Asoka is pretending to be us. Like so much of Buddhism, this strikes me as

curiously sane and compelling even if a child can make an appo-
site counter argument, substituting "Mickey Mouse" or "Lucy the
Unicorn" for Buddha. The issue comes down to this: does a Buddha
embody profound qualifies of "actual" mindfulness, which is Rilke's
beautiful argument for the existence of unicorns.* It is no doubt a
karmic flaw in my make-up that I find his demonstration compelling because poetic and Palmo's weak, because *religious*. (* *"In fact,
it never was. Yet because they loved it, a pure creature happened. It
always had space and in that space, clear and left open, it easily raised
its head and hardly needed to become, fed with no grain, only with
the possibility that it might be."* Rilke, *Sonnets to Orpheus, no.4.)*

No one alive for the last fifty years can really comprehend the history of that time; we don't know the secrets. Those that come after
won't understand it either, even in possession of the revelations.
They won't have had the feelings.

All of us understand already the driving forces of human acts:
fear, aggression, ambition, envy, stupidity, boredom and misunder-
standing. And let's not forget the better elements from this Pandora's
box of bad motivations, hope and helpfulness. (All expostulated
in Homer, the best of historians who says, for starters, "The gods
decided and ordained unto men ordeal and destruction that no
age would lack for song.")

Because some say there are gods, angels, platonic forms and others
say there are no gods, angels and platonic forms, our best philosophy is an open grasp of contradiction as when in dreams we are
both here and there, speak to one person who is two, see a small,
inquiring animal that is absolute cat and definitive dog.

Since the greatest physical pleasure is sex, it's no wonder even the
aged keep doing it as long as they can. Youth, understandably,

regards coitus among the elderly as deviant and unaesthetic. (For instance, we can hardly even contemplate the categorical companion to "dirty old men", "nasty old women".) The greatest *mental* pleasure is artistic creation, with rhythms and exhalations resembling sex which explains why artists can't stop producing even though their last works usually have all the utility and beauty of geriatric sex. (The reverence accorded burnout old artists is one the scandals of the age.)

Confucius say: "When the daily news means nothing and the latest free offer – warm water cruise, soft breezes doesn't entice because the next Big Thing you are looking forward to (wait for it … knuckle bone drum) isn't sex or praise but Death, isn't it time you staggered towards the sunset, chum?"

Special Pleading. Though we probably agree on the definition and the estimation of those qualities lacking from my work, your calling it "disorganized' makes me blush and utter "Oh, no, no, no" not as denial, rather in modest resistance of too fine a complement since "completed" works have a finish that glosses over the component tonalities in the manner of a person telling you intelligent things always in the same cultivated tone of voice. Lawrence, for once, was right, "There is charm in chaos not reduced to order." Even the master craftsman Heaney graciously concedes "Imperfection has its prerogatives."

Just as common men know what they cannot believe, that they are mortal, so average artists know but cannot credit their mediocrity. All life and most creativity occurs in this gap between Knowledge and Belief. The few who narrow it, exhilarated rather than suffocated by truth, are not, for that alone, better artists or superior persons.

As a writer, he was seriously disabled by sincerity.

The most discouraging thing after a hard night is hearing the birds singing their paeans to the inevitable day. The most encouraging thing after a hard night is hearing the birds singing their paeans to the renewing day.

Increasingly, I lack the mental energy for understanding my life, why certain things happened, why I am this rather than that kind of person; my mind wanders, I get nowhere. If I falter in the study of the thing I should know best, my own life, it's no surprise that I make no headway on the big issues: truth, morality, art. I'm simply not up to it (when I was, young and capable of powerful thought, most of that drive was misdirected by sex), a person struggling with a puzzle so intractable he loses interest. Not that we should accept this state of stasis. There is a set of answers. It's just we are hardly ever up to it.

People think about death as a grim generality headed their way or contemplate particular cases, Old Uncle Ned, dead. What they cannot bear because it is humiliating is the apprehension of the invincible details, a button of malignancy mobbing the delicate pancreas, how a little clog overthrows all one's big ambitions, grand passions and elaborate routines, rendering one of interest only to pathologists, purposive and attractive persons we should admire in the way in-play amateurs always admire the real professionals; in this case, abstracters of death in detail.

That god became human to make a blood sacrifice to redeem our sins strikes me as barbarically absurd. What makes sense is that god, who made us as we are on a planet where the slope of nature doesn't rise to the good, died to a pay *his* debt of sin, not ours.

Being a sensitive chap, seeing that the world He made was a home construction project gone so wrong it could only be destroyed or abnegatedly resigned to, He decided to kill himself. That is, he embodied himself as human and allowed us to kill him at a date no later than the Holocaust. Angels are still with us, cold intelligences that take an occasional non-interventionary interest in us like birds looking through a pane of glass.

The exhibition of classical Japanese armor displayed the usual exquisite forms and finishes, high aesthetics that is a high achievement. No wonder such a culture would have the confidence to adopt and adapt anything, especially mere material technologies
    [Editor's note. Nelson here inserts a trans-
lated section from the purported Pillow Book of
Lady Soitghoesie, a contemporary of Sei Shonagon
and Murasaki.]

Unpleasant Things

A woman who bears in her body one lover's seed to another. Disgusting.

A lover who complains of inconsequential things damaging the friendship, such as not having a book ready for lending, when he is secretly the special friend of another.

A person at dinner who praises the character of his lover when everyone else at the table knows she is false. His ignorance has made it awkward for everyone. How embarrassing.

People who smile while lying.

Death is a mystery we cannot understand; a greater one is the expiration of love. The person you would have given your life for is now one you don't even bother to cross the street to avoid. What chemistry makes these hard hearts?

The renowned writer says what must be rejected is the natural tendency of the pen to produce superficialities, glib aesthetics and shallow superiority. Good writers work hard to scale down these effects. The rarest "Middle Way" would be to accept and accentuate such natural flaws, leaving the scribal wood exposed, burnished and developed to the point of luster.

No poet has been more contemptuous of the pretensions of poets than yours truly, a forthright, self-awarded distinction. (As to poetry itself, can it set an arm, a leg, dress a wound? No. It's mere words. What are words? Breath.) Yet they should take legitimate pride that identically to pilots in their myriad gradations, they have graduated from ground level and operate in the elements of air and Aerial.

The Perfect Hurt. The damage must be real enough to deform the natural egotistical conceits ("I am worthy, lucky, winning, attractive, right") but not so destructive, as is often the case, to annihilate identity. Tending the injury, one acquires depth and maturity that is the basis of real (rather than facile) understanding and sympathy. While one should resist viewing this entire process too self-congratulatorily – "Now, I am wise, compassionate, etc.", life always has a way of ballasting such resilient buoyancy.

The past is both the destroyer and progenitor of futures. It is one thing to be defeated by external forces, other to be self-vanquished by insisting on what cannot be. For example, the person who, correctly, insists that the Holocaust must not happen and because it has, rejects any good that is associated with it such as Jewish life in the state of Israel. Or the highly moral person who insists that American slavery should never have happened and because it did is curiously allied with the judicious southerner who can't be reconciled to anything as heroically resistant as the Confederacy being defeated and so both despise the United States. While the great national issues (and I have known these expositing persons) illuminate the general dynamic, the most acute instances are always the intimate and personal.

Ah, Shucks. The perfect book for me is not a beautiful verbal animal (Rilke's private unicorn or indeed his entire lovely corpus) but a hard, almost disagreeable excrescence one cuts thorough in increasingly desperate (and diminishing) expectation of the glistening pearl.

Macbeth, appraising the hags' prophecies, concludes they "cannot be ill, cannot be good." In regard to the supernatural soliciting of art, Macbeth the critic would have said "cannot be false, cannot be true". Art is the great equivocation, the witches the nearest conjuration to artists.

There must have been a no later than date when everyone should have seen the British Empire was finished, done, "cooked', ridiculous as the prancing plumes in the viceroy's hat. But the gracious retirement came very late, the 1950s. As to America, the next great thing is already stirring, ready for its bloody birth. Do we see?

A young man in his vitality cannot comprehend death. To have knowledge of it, some will risk their lives in the military or dangerous sports or extensively read as I did about exotic deaths, people dying in submarines or on mountain slopes. Death could only be understood in the intensity of its extremer range. As one gets older, death seems a friend, as familiar as going to bed, as blandly exceptional as not getting up one morning, the double irony being that having seen people die, one knows it is like being born, hard and common.

We are mistaken to say out lives are too short (unless from accident or disease, they are). Short compared to what, a rat, a cat, a horse? What is short is the scope of our lives. We sense vast time before and after, conceive of millions of unfathomable fates. Our personal expanse is small. In that space, we curate the present and the past. What experience could possibly qualify us for such a task? For that, our lives *are* too short.

Most people just want to be happy. A few want to be hurt and won't be "happy" until they are. Happily, the world is so constituted they are certain of being gratified.

Persons that shun success lest it prove the ultimate disappointment are the same type that can find sufficient satisfaction in failure even, rather especially if, they must search for it.

I wasn't disconsolated by my rival receiving deserved praise from real persons when all my commendation was contrived, from persons I'd made up, because my fictional admirers were more beautiful and insightful than her real ones could ever be.

Certain events so determine a life they must constantly be revisited if one is to live authentically. Yet the range at which they illuminate is also where they incinerate. One is in constant oscillation between safety and identity. Persons in this situation will be least at ease with the fixed positions of conventionally and are, to that extent, artists.

We've all seen on TV the mother of the murdered child who forgives the killer. Having the unbearable burden of immense pain and hate, she has taken advantage of one means, forgiveness, to make her life endurable. Nobler is holding the hurt and the hate yet doing no harm. Because revenge is often criminal, because always it is rough justice that reverses the polarity of innocence and guilt, because its lash distracts the perpetrators from the common mire of their lives.

In novels, "Jim" may, for example, marry Susan or Jill or Mary, all of them or none, move to Nepal, fly to Mars. It is this kind of evolution in freedom that makes literature trivial.

In novels, "Jim" may, for example, marry Susan or Jill or Mary, all of them or none, move to Nepal, fly to Mars. It is this kind of evolution in freedom that makes literature important. [Editor's note: The author has stipulated that these are two independent observations, not one that is bifurcated.]

At the highest level, the difference between first rate second rate minds such as Sartre and Heidegger and second rate first rate ones such as Nietzsche, is geometrical, not arithmetical, the former like a short bayonet stabbing again and again at the heart of truth which the latter, sword like, cleaves with a single thrust.

Contradictum: Nietzsche's definitions of "woman" are sitcom comedic only they aren't comedy. And despite being anti-anti-Semitic at least when he was sane, he is guilty for starting a train of thought – Jews are responsible for Christianity and Christianity is a debilitating morality that must be overcome – which terminates at Auschwitz-Birkenau not Valhalla-Asgaard.

We gather our life's gems and dark pearls. They are non-temporal, solid conceptual objects. If we string them together in narrative to make a kind of necklace, meaningful as any made thing, Simon is right too to loop the strand back and rearrange the facets of event since, in no particular order, we finger them daily for the intensity of the touch. [Editor's note: This passage may account for the otherwise inexplicable addition of gem and mineral names to the list of Contents.]

What haunts me at the end of my life isn't personal defeats or "roads not taken". It's that even five minutes of my precious human life was by occupied by bad TV, junk music, trash films, unintelligent books and stupid chat, an inexcusable expense of spirit in a waste of shame.

My interest in death isn't morbid but a curiosity about the vast majority of the world's creatures, the living being a small, hyperactive minority. The obvious options: the dead are existent (in reborn bodies or as souls) or they are not. Let's instead propose a state that transcends all our categories of existence and non existence, a thing utterly strange we can say nothing about it, a compelling argument since nothing can refute silence.

I am often tempted to say to my Buddhist friends "The West also has a complex system of mediation. It's called literature."

In Venice there is a beautiful little bridge, the smallest suspension of disbelief type in the world, spanning fifteen feet of murky green canal to connect the quarters of Santa Maria Maddalena and Gatto nel Vicolo. You need to own that bridge. And there's this gal, this guy I'd like you to meet. One right up your canali.

After four decades of paying attention to one part of his body (the penis), a man is ready for serenity and wisdom. But all the organs he was neglecting now clamor for attention, some insistently, "Give me some thought or I will kill you." And he does. "Give me some thought and I will kill you." And it does.

In the next life, we may be as grounded and intuitive, as right as a stone. In this life, cultivate the magnifying flaw of self-consciousness which, like tuning a microscope, gives so great a clarity in the sudden instance of over-focus one must, for continuance, turn away. We are sharpened to know. (from *Zen and Tonic*).

Humor of the death certificate – the one document you will never have to prove you've earned.

The Sociology of Adultery. In Germany, Switzerland, it is a mere social fact, in Scandinavia it's routine, in France and Italy, a nice recreation (for males), in Britain, Canada, America it is as common and need be no more tragic than knee surgery. In a long life I've known five betrayed partners; all said it was the worst event of their lives, two averred they had rather been murdered. Which

141

argues that except for a few spots in Europe, adultery should never be taken or undertaken lightly even if in developed countries its literary prospect is no longer tragedy but satire – one sounding a bit tinny as long as even one person is killed (generally but not exclusively "the guilty") or injured because of sexually infidelity. Ladies and gentlemen, get used to it; ours is a bawdy planet.

Intensely condemned or honored when you do not deserve it, loving someone you wish you didn't, surviving something you wish you hadn't, these are common contradictions which if strong enough condition a life; you wouldn't change things even if you could and you can't. One has transitioned from living a contradiction to a living contradiction.

A vibrating part will destroy an engine unless the whole mechanical block begins to shake in sync, a matter of resolution, not solution.

At the reading, the poet articulates each word he has written with a reverence and self-wondrousness that makes one's nose itch. Pure words may deserve our respect but spoken in our mouths, they return to common use and ask for nothing more than honest, unaffected utterance. (In other words, don't embarrass them or yourself by pointing and making awe-struck gestures when they are trying to get to work.)

Formula for history. It feels good to be good but it feels better to be victorious.

In a complex world of right and wrong actions, shouldn't we thank god for revenge since by its action, victims are released from the utterly hell of inert suffering. It restoreth thy soul, it leadth thee to green pastures, thy cup runneth over. Which is the problem: revenge is usually rough justice with a plutonium like excess that powers an entire grid of new transgression. If forgiveness voids this entanglement, it also, as Shylock so cogently argues, subverts justice. (How presumptuous of uninjured Portia to preach mercy!) Unless the injured freely rejects vengeance. Where are we then? Are the perps moved to reformation? Are they prevented? True, an eye for an eye makes the world blind. Yet "a tooth for a tooth" not only lessens the bite of the bad but keeps good dentists in business.

Glib? We are moral beings and can do better than retributive reaction. But before any of you, Mr. Buddhist, Miss Christian, Mr. and Mrs. Humanist prohibit this redressive drug in every case, consider Vengeance's clarifying effects, its gratifying action. How can anything so natural not be good? "Vengeance is mine saith the Lord" isn't so much a prohibition as one hell of a product placement. Which is not to say it isn't desirable to cultivate compassion as a personal refinement since the person who decides "to even the score" seldom knows the score and is operating from an ignorance no less than that which made him vulnerable to begin with except that now being willed, it retrospectively justifies his injury. The only advance comes in admitting you don't know the score. You don't even know the game.

My hope was that between the devastating something and Death's final laying down of arms, there was ground for tactical battle, small victories that could make my name.

In evaluating art, the words "arrogant" and "lazy" may generally be used interchangeably. This is an aesthetic truism and to such the same rubric applies.

There is no personal achievement in having insights about Shakespeare because Shakespeare is an insight generating machine. Yet I must offer one in conservation of a play I much admire, *Much Ado About Nothing*. The play's climax is not the tremendously affecting abortive wedding but what happens shortly after when Beatrice, in response to Benedict's query of how he may serve her, says "Kill Claudio". Shakespeare is headlong here, making a scene not for spectators to view or share in shock but to experience in the instant of their own existence. Many modern audiences can't catch up, they can only process her urging as a joke and in the long short moment of their laugher miss the play's ultimate transpiring: for it is then, removed from all jests, flirtations and wars of wit that Beatrice and Benedict are most real to one another; more exposed in their naked being than later they will be in their bodies (he, a soldier and a gentleman, has known many women). It may not matter at all or it may a great deal that in the extreme disjuncture of her request, she penetrates him.

Wildlife: animals that mind their own business. *Modesty:* the most insidious of conceits. *Trust:* a type of mental lassitude. *Friends:* familiars you know how to lie to. *Heritage:* grave robbery to bedeck the naked present. *Pride:* dress armor, weaker than it looks. *Poet:* polite term for the under-employed. *Praise:* a slow poison administered by the envious. *Tolerance:* lack of conviction … The one line "zinger": a sleight of hand like slight of mind, with the virtue of speed and a trick's quota of truth. *Self-critique:* self-congratulation.

If we lived forever, we could continue in our contentions; the gods never forget and only forgive contingently and tactically. Because we are mortal, we need to leave our rancors on the near shore if on the other we are to be spared, as beings of lessened gravity not yet of grace, self lacerating abrasions against the hard trammels of our retained hate. (All speculation about the afterlife springs from our being in the habit of living.)

To take a not quite serious take on what is most serious, this is the bend of the bow. And after the arrow's shot, what? The hum of the string.

It was a movement of mental music (Mendelssohnian and Schumannic, shifting and in motion), describing a slope that inclined me to a dimensionality "hurt" and searching.

The Garden. After the hard time of thrust and cut, aching from the spades, when we'd had enough and couldn't do anymore, breathing deeply, we saw what we had made – a space for light and air where everything growing was our own.

Were it known that the only existing copy of this book is the one you hold in your hands, would it have more value?

Personal Epilogues

Charles Carsen. Born in Aurora N,Y, of Mormon parents, the young Carsen was mathematically gifted and received a full scholarship to attended the University of Virginia where he majored in mathematics and philosophy, studying with Edward Thompson, one of Wittgenstein's last students, who encouraged Carsen's postgraduate work at St John's College, Cambridge where he received his PhD in1970.

Returning to Virginia as an assistant professor, his book "*The Logical Calculus of Ethics*" was the second volume published in Cambridge's prestigious "Problems of Philosophy" series and earned him tenure in1974. Despite its ingenuity, the book's strong Platonic bias meant it had little influence on philosophical discourse. Carsen never wrote another. A revered teacher, he received the student-awarded "Best Teacher Award" in 1980, 1998, 2000 and 2010, tying the University's record for this recognition.

Sepadra Chopad (aka Karen Summers). Affirming her lesbian identity with an involvement with a graduate student whom she followed to Naropa University in Boulder Colorado, Karen began an intense study of Buddhism, completing her ngondro preliminaries in 1986 (100,000 prostrations, mandalla offerings and refuge vows under the tutelage of her root guru, Trangue Tulku concluded just prior to his untimely death from alcoholism.) After five years in Boulder, Karen, now Sepadra Chopad, took preliminary vows at the Gampo Nunnery in Nova Scotia and was later fully ordained, becoming associate Abbess in 1996 and Honorable Abbess (Shraragampa) four years later. She is a much sought after mentor and speaker in Buddhist circles and is the author of *A Flower Opening: Tantra for Women* and (with Judah Levine) *Madramudra Manual* (Shamballa)

Vera Fielder. Following her break up with […], [Editor's Note. A proper name is lacking in the text.] Vera moved to California where she taught freshmen composition at the Stanford University. There she encountered Richard Leppard, an undergraduate acquaintance at their alma mater (the University of Michigan) and now Exxon Mobile professor of Geophysics. Within a year they married. Mother of two college-age children, Vera is a popular teacher and the author of *Schnauzer: Training Your Super Dog.*

Moses Mahone is lay pastor of the Independent Free Will Assembly of God, in Front Royal, Virginia.

Guy Maximilian Mantis. Guy was married to Adhalla Mourturki, a graduate student from Turkey in 1988. With Masters degrees from UVa, they taught English at Ismail University in Istanbul for two years before returning to the United States. They subsequently took positions at The Summit School, an elite private academy outside of Mobile where Guy taught studio art until his suspension for sexual harassment. Setting up a private studio, Mantis has had a successful career and is an important regional artist in the humid crescent from Houston to Tallahassee, specializing in the production of large scale abstract murals for bank and hotel lobbies, corporate board rooms and bar-bistro décor. The father of three sons, he is at the time of this writing, separated (not divorced) from his wife.

Janet Nielson. After a decade's enrollment (full and part-time) in graduate study Classics at the University of Virginia, Janet withdrew from the program, abandoning at near completion her dissertation, *Forked Paths: Duplicity and Truth in the Drama of Euripides.* She is currently an editor and copy writer in the Publications Department of Bardolph College, Lynchburg Virginia. Her husband is a cataloger in the college's Constance Bumbles Library and the author of *A Wilderness of Monkeys*, *Trooping the Colour* and other assorted volumes. Now (2014) marking 30 years of official marriage, they are regarded by friends and colleagues as a compatible and comfortable couple who have not done all they might.

Rafer Sampson. Sampson retired from the NFL after eight seasons, playing with the Detroit Bangals and Baltimore Bolts, appearing in two Super Bowels; he was twice runner up for the league's most valuable player. He retired to Charlottesville, opened Rafer's Grill and became increasingly involved in local real-estate and social issues. Rafer was elected to city council in 1994 and 1998, becoming mayor in 2002, for one term. A self-taught saxophonist, he has jammed with The Rave Mathews Band, and appears on their album *"Rail Tracks Twilight."*

William Ruminant. Following graduate study at the Universities of Michigan and Virginia, he taught at Yale before being appointed Director of the Institute for Writing (later the William Ruminant Institute for Textual and Editorial Studies, or WRITES) at Edmister University where he is Founder's (formerly Verver) Professor of Comparative Literature. He is the author of numerous articles and books, among them *After the Fire* (Ohio University Press) and *Pretext — a Manual for Editing in the Postmodern Era* (Harvard University Press). He was Alcan-Sorel Docente-Visiteur Distingue at the Universite de Paris (IV) for the 2012-2013 term.

Introduction by Willam Ruminant.

What is it that makes a thing self-identical with itself and recognizable by others? We think we know what a poem is but many poems are prose, what constitutes a novel yet cannot define how it can accommodate forms as diverse as *Clarissa* and *The Unnamable*. These same questions arise in science, philosophy and life. Who is it that does the things that makes us who we are?

As Rudolph Gasche observes with typical clarity and concision, "The unity of the whole stems from an articulation (Gefuge), a relationship and connection of the parts. No wonder then that Flach stresses the themes of combination, communion or interlacing in technical terms *koinonia* and *symploke* and that he conceives of this heterology as an essential freeing of the idea of *symploke* to include otherness, in this case linking into One the hierological and the homogeneous realm of judgment, the domain of the absolutely different ground and the domain of what is grounded as well as the idea of unity itself. Flach asks in what manner does heterology come to grips with the problem of *symploke*? In the only sufficient one, namely by conceiving unity, difference, totality as foundation in their unifiability as the uniform and unified speculative character of the absolute relation. Which comprises the One and the Other in which the Other is not the negation of the One but an exclusive Other of the same."

This mirrors the profound insight of Bhan Jho Strum, the initiating archivist-philosopher of the 17th century Pali renaissance, who asked in a classic formulation that is a foundational study of every graduate student at WRITES "What is a text? It cannot be any one element, nor is it the sum ('Shebob") of elements, nor is it the action. It is an imputation of mind."

That texts provide us with the perfectly contained and clinically friendly model for studying indeed formulating the "deeper" problems of Dasein is one of the profoundest satisfactions of literature and a platitude. Ideally, as the text is clarified, consciousness is intricated, the literary object being a dense particle exponentially exfoliating into an expansive cosmos of realizations. Not withstanding the potential wrapped up in the difficulty, Nelson's manuscript, which he termed "literary mixed-media", presented us with distinct obstacles since its self subversions occur at diverse and non-symmetrical levels: first that of overtly contradictory and hence non-contradictory utterance; secondly, a discomfiture and misfit of forms. Finally, a personal failure of technique and control.

We know from ancillary documents that the object we have in hand is at most only two thirds completed. On the morning of April 15th 2013, Nelson complained to his long time companion Janet Nielson of heart palpitations, vertigo and headache, asking her to accompany him as he walked the three blocks to the nearby Massachusetts General Hospital. Suspecting stroke, emergency room physicians conducted an immediate EKG and CAT scan. Results were negative and after several hours of observation, he was released. Follow-up diagnostics with an MRI revealed a small (.5 cm) sarcastic neuroma on the auditory nerve, accounting for the vertigo and which required monitoring. Otherwise, he was in good health. Yet he stopped work on *A Book of Emblems*. To date he has not resumed writing of any kind.

The evidence of loss of control is methodological. His original intent was to take Johann De Brune's *Embelmata of Zinn-Werck* of 1636 and devise a series of free-form essays inspired by Adriaen van de Venne's iconic and accomplished engravings. This intention was fulfilled only through the course of five essays totaling twenty-five pages. After, the work was increasingly determined (undermined) by a sporadically episodic account of a set of young lovers and an ensuing "adultery", loosely termed.

Van de Venne's engravings were no longer generative of texts but deployed as simple illustrations. Nothing in his prior work, *A Wilderness of Monkeys* and *Trooping the Colour*, demonstrated any compatibility with the achievement of a consistent, coherent and extended narrative. The author was increasingly torn between a tantalizing variety of compelling approaches; that of the fictional

– the evolving in free thought of antimoniel concerns towards a formal resolution that for lack of a better term can be called "the Beautiful."; the historical – the rendering and refining of actuality into Truth, and lastly, the philosophical-aphoristical, visionary if verbal incisions that reveal the real.

From textual and documentary analysis it is clear Nelson worked in all modes simultaneously modulated in four voices, the wry, the accusatory, the plaintive, the resolved (both as will and closure).

Imagination resists the tyranny of the real. Artistic form sculpts historical content into philosophical truth. Nelson, alas, dissipated his emancipating vision in a murky dimension compounded of reality and delusion. We know from the reliable testimony of the author's close friend, Guy Mantis, that many of the recorded events never occurred. Technically challenged, baffled by an esthetic terrain alien to his navigational instincts, suspended between the possibilities of invention and the strictures of history, Nelson couldn't go on and one chill spring morning, he didn't. One might wonder he got as far as he did, this unreliably kaironic writer purgatorially shape-shifting along a baroquen syntagmatic line.

We have dwelt for purposes of conventional introduction too long in the biographisphere where molar subjects wager for complicity on the biased basis of transcendental identities. That the facts of a life influence the form of art is certainly valid at the most accessible of Delueze's one thousand plateaus. At a higher altitude, the artist as persona, however conditioned, is free (we are all born into a language and deploy it divergently) in the operations of his art. This is the entire topic of traditional criticism in all its expatiations.

At WRITES, our main investigation is survey of another, non personal realm for which the old post modernist bromide "texts write themselves" if not a definitive designation of destination does point in the right direction. Here, texts in their vast variety and deep receptivity interact in a strange physics, with reactions, transformations and unpredictable effects that have nothing to do with the individual aside from her being a kind of petrie dish, a locality for the culture of event. Our "author" was repelled by the boundaries circumscribing existing literary forms: the historical fictional, the fictional historical and everything in between. While aware of such radical departures as *The Unnamable* – a non novel (offspring of Joyce) about a non subject, even these missiles, avante-gardes, seemed to him never despite their tracable ascent to have escaped the common gravity of what-you'd-expect, engendering his responsive reactions, his variations between this and that as if the velocity of alteration would describe like atomic orbits, a new apparitional object.

To say that Nelson initiated and defined a novel genre-object, "literary mixed media" would be both true, false and consistent with his equivocations which if they are to be explicated can only be by another ambiguity of at least two terms exfoliating into four more branchings, an expansive network, not an explanative object, an expostulation of a co-dependent, co-existing verbal biosphere, justified as life, by its vitality and that alone.

The Word file came to us at WRITES in three separate versions, the chapters in highly variant disorder and, as expected from our prior engagement with *Wilderness of Monkeys* and *Trooping the Colour*, with many typographical errors and multiple mis-formattings that needed to be distinguished from neologisms and other "intentional" imputations. It became the primary topic subject of that semester's "Traces and Transcriptions" seminar, one of WRITE's introductory advanced practicums in forensic editing. At the end of four months, we had a product that could be evaluated for appearance in the Institute's *Pretexts* series. Fortuitously, we were also in contact with Another Sparrow, a small, culturally cognizant press with which we have successfully collaborated on many occasions. It found *A Book of Emblems* publishable, the author's companion, with power of attorney, approving its transfer. Why did anyone bother?

An anecdote from the life of Bhan Jho Strum, recorded by his pupils, may be relevant and revelatory: "And as our guru readied to leave the court along the path to the wilderness, a student cried "Master, will you not miss the perfumed and painted chambers, the dance of the beautiful maidens, the discourses with wise men, the sound of delightful music?" He said unto them "All these are music and the deepest music lives in the forest."

We detect an echoing harmonic in the words of another mage who died a hemisphere away about the time of Sturm's birth, "the isle is full of noises, sounds and sweet airs." Nelson's tempestic conjurations never congeal into entity or island. They are aligned as verbal reefs, shoals, bars, contingently emergent turbulences that lapped by fluid attention, emit curious noises, sensible if shallow aires.

Acknowledgments

A book of this type could not exist without the support of many individuals and institutions. The author is compelled to thank, in order roughly proportionate to their contribution: Open Library for making available the Emblemata of Zinne-werck; Dr. William Ruminant, his staff (especially Naomi Roth) and students at The William Ruminate Institute of Textual and Editorial Studies (WRITES), Edmister University; my faithful friends, Bosco Woods and Mona Crumpett; the staff and collections of the University of Virginia Library; the staff and collections of Harvard University Library; Dr Dee Faustus of Harvard's Barabbas Extension School who gave a troubled young man another chance; Hamilton Burger, Reference Librarian at Boston College School of Law Library for needful legal research; Alphonse Dominique de Villepin Bone who not only generously provided access and guidance to his great-great-grandfather's archives but was a tireless resource on all matters military; Professor Jack Van der Mule and Dr. Janet (no relation) Nielson, translators of texts vital for the book's composition; for promotional and public relations expertise essential in today's publishing environment, Fred Netschau at Zarathustra Inc.; for gifts in kind and donated services, Bauer Wines (Boston), Hestar Stables (Iceland) and Grigory "Gig" Lenovo (computer-support, Charlottesville); last but not least, the bold flock at Another Sparrow who picked up and flew with a project no other press would even peck at.

Coda

We enter the airy oblong box,
Symphony Hall's expectant space
framed by tons of bricks, plaster, iron
sitting atop 20,000 white pine pilings
driven deep into the muddy bottom.
Check the ticket; we are high up
second balcony left, 22 and 23B
and soon on the edge of our seats
to see the conductor and because this is exciting stuff –
the finish, trombone golden, of Schumann's "Rhenish",
a bright island of sound surrounded
by cosmic static, white noise of the stars
and eighty meters beneath us,
the waters of an ancient lake,
cold, still, color of slate.

www.ingramcontent.com/pod-product-compliance
Lightning Source LLC
Chambersburg PA
CBHW051828170626
46807CB00003B/1083